ASTAROTH'S
INFERNAL
LEGIONS

Other works by Sean G. McAnulty

Dracula Vs Cthulhu... Sort Of
And Other Stories

Kali The Werewolf

Grath The Noble Demon and Clive The Necromancer

Vepar's Infernal Legions

ASTAROTH'S INFERNAL LEGIONS

A LESBIAN IN TRANSYLVANIA

Sean G. McAnulty

Illustrations by

Anastacia Bond
&
Jen Forth

ASTAROTH'S INFERNAL LEGIONS

Published by Sean G. McAnulty, Nanaimo, Canada

ISBN
Paperback   978-1-77354-477-9
eBook   978-1-77354-544-8

Publication assistance by

PUBLISHING
PageMaster.ca

CONTENTS

CHAPTER ONE

The Romanian Carpathian Mountains were beautiful in August. They provided a breathtaking view of the countryside, itself a vision of wonder that wouldn't be out of place in a children's fairy tale. Standing at the right spot, one would see rich forests lining lush verdant meadows. These meadows were dotted with rustic old-fashioned houses only found in small town Eastern Europe. New highways connected with old trails to provide a juxtaposition of modern convenience and ancient tradition. These pathways, old and new, were lined with wildflowers that bloomed under the blue summer sky. It was a beautiful place, and Debbie was happy to be able to share it with her girlfriend May.

It's the little details that make an experience memorable. The sound of Debbie's Kawasaki Ninja H2 SX purring as they ascended the mountain road. The feeling of May's arms around Debbie's waist, suggesting vulnerability, but also trust. The cool breeze that wafted through Debbie's short hair as she parked her bike under the shade of a maple tree. The distant sounds of birds chirping as the women followed a shady path to a clearing with a view of the valley below. The softness of a blanket's fabric as Debbie and May spread it over the grass of the clearing. Finally, the easy relaxation as the young women stretched out on said blanket. These little details helped make Debbie and May's picnic date special.

The two women had only been dating for a short period of time, but when you felt a connection with the right person time didn't really matter. All Debbie had to do was look into May's captivating eyes to know that they had something special. The fact that the two women were so different wasn't an issue; after all, opposites attract. May was a 5'4" Romanian girl, with shoulder length black hair, and green eyes. Debbie was a 5'9" Canadian girl of Irish heritage, with short brown hair and grey eyes. Normally Debbie was the more assertive and confident of the two women, while May was shy and timid. But lately May had been coming out of her shell a little bit. Debbie liked to think she had helped bring out May's hidden potential. When the two women were alone together, Debbie was happy to see May take the initiative. This date, for example, had been May's idea.

"I have surprise for you." May said, as the two women relaxed on the blanket. The Romanian girl spoke with a thick accent, but she had a reasonably firm command of English. "Close your eyes."

"That's asking a lot, given what we've been through." Debbie teased. Though the last few days had been a blur, Debbie was sure there had been a few crazy moments here and there. The recently bandaged cut on her hand was proof of that much. But it didn't really matter. Debbie trusted her girlfriend and closed her eyes.

"OK, open them now, please."

Debbie opened her eyes and saw May had placed a binder between the two women. "What's this?"

"I make scrapbook for you." May said. "Little things, from the relationship. I promise myself that I give it to you at one of the perfect moments. Right now, we have picnic with seeing my hometown on this beautiful sunny day. I think to myself that this is perfect moment."

Debbie saw May blush as she spoke. This was clearly a gesture of intimacy and trust. Debbie opened the binder to the first page and saw a cup sleeve taped to the page. The object triggered a previous memory. "I remember this. This is the first time we met."

***

Debbie and Simon grimaced as they made the transition from the hot summer weather outside to the air conditioned '5 to Go' coffee shop. They had been riding their motorcycles most of the day, separate from the rest of their touring group. 'European Chopper Experiences' or ECE, was an online group that had attracted Debbie's notice. The group promised a motorcycle tour of Europe with experienced guides that provided the best bargains for the area. It offered a new experience for a young woman fresh out of university. A young woman eager to see more of the world. The only downside was the group mostly consisted of men, as fewer women had a passion for motorcycles. But Debbie could handle that. She was an open lesbian, but that didn't stop her from being friends with men. For instance, she had quickly formed a friendship with Simon.

Simon Johnston stood out from the other bikers of the touring group by being unusually short, with a height of only 5'2". Additionally, Simon was more timid than the other men in ECE, shy and withdrawn. Debbie had taken a liking to him immediately. She had made her sexuality clear from the start, so Simon wouldn't get the wrong idea, but since she was new to the group she was eager to make new friends. Just a few days of speaking to Simon had caused him to warm to her considerably. Often, they broke away from the main group to tour the European countryside together. Now they were in Romania, in a 5 to Go, and Debbie was thirsty.

"Could I get an iced coffee with extra milk?" Debbie asked as she approached the counter.

"It's on me." Simon said. "And I'll get a smoothie."

"Oh, you didn't have to do that." Debbie said. She hadn't asked Simon to pay for her drink. In fact, she felt a little uncomfortable that he had been so forward with the idea. But they were friends, and perhaps that was just what friends did. "I'll get the next one then."

"What kind of smoothie?" The young woman behind the counter asked. The voice was heavily accented but spoke fluent English. Debbie found herself grateful that there was a younger person behind the counter. There was a myth that everyone in Europe spoke English. This was not true, not at all. The younger generation was more likely to be fluent in the language, but there were many who would respond to a question in English with a blank stare. Touring the continent, Debbie found Europe was overall not that different from her home. But once in a while she would find herself alone with someone who did not speak her language. When that moment came, Debbie would be reminded that she was a stranger in a foreign country.

"I'll take strawberry." Simon said. He paid the young woman behind the counter and went to find a table. Debbie looked beyond the counter and her eyes locked with eyes that shone a brilliant green. Eye contact is a simple but effective form of communication. Not a word is spoken in such an exchange, yet it is an intimate experience. Debbie saw the server blush and quickly turn away, but in that one moment she had felt a real connection. A moment of true beauty. It was with extreme reluctance that Debbie walked away from the counter and joined Simon at his table.

"Simon, you said you're from Seattle, right?" Debbie asked. She still felt a little stricken from the moment she'd just experienced. But she wasn't a little kid, she was 23 now, a grown woman. She could control herself just fine.

"I'm actually from Bellevue." Simon said. "But Seattle is more widely known so I just name that city for simplicity's sake. Sometimes you don't want to go into the nitty gritty details of exactly where a place is, you know what I mean?"

"Sure." Debbie said. Her reply had been perfunctory. Debbie wasn't really eager to talk about where Simon was from. She had just wanted to make some small talk as she brought herself back to reality. Why was she suddenly so crazy over making eye contact with some girl in a coffee shop? Even as these thoughts went through her mind, she saw the same girl carrying their drinks to their table.

"Hi, sorry, did you-." The girl never had an opportunity to finish. Timid, shy, and perhaps with her own distractions, the server misstepped. Debbie had been overheated by the warm summer's day. At once she was cooled by an application of iced coffee and strawberry smoothie as both beverages spilled on her. "Oh no! Oh, I am so sorry! Your shirt, let me help you." The young woman grabbed Debbie by her arm and pulled her to her feet. Debbie was already thrown off guard by the sudden chill of the drinks. But the touch of the young woman on top of that threw her for a loop. The young server's hands on her arm were soft and warm. Gentle, but with a nervous energy. Debbie's eyes fell to a name tag on the woman's chest. Maia, the server's tag said Maia.

The server guided Debbie to a backroom of the coffee shop. The young woman saw shelves containing cups, coffee powder, creamers, and packets of flavouring. On another shelf she saw uniforms and merchandise. Beyond these shelves Debbie saw a sink, a washer and a dryer. Debbie took in all of this in a heartbeat as the server began gesturing to the sink. She appeared flustered, unable to speak. "Hey Maia, it's not a big deal." Debbie took off her shirt and handed it to the server in one fluid motion.

"It's May." The server said. But even as she spoke the young woman blushed and turned away from Debbie.

"OK sure, May it is. Why are you suddenly so bashful?" Debbie asked. As she spoke, she looked down at her chest, now clad in a sports bra. Debbie had an impressive physique, the body of an amateur athlete.

Brought about by the fact that she ran cross country as a hobby. She ran an hour in the morning and if she was in the mood, an additional hour as the sun set. Yet she didn't see why this should be a concern for May. "Look May, what's the issue? I'm a girl, you're a girl. I don't have anything you haven't seen already."

"Perhaps, this might help, please?" May said, offering a coffee shop apron to Debbie. Debbie looked at the slim article of clothing dubiously. It was relatively thin and wouldn't cover too much of her torso. Her sports bra would still be quite visible. But if it made May feel more comfortable, she didn't mind putting it on.

"Sure, whatever you like." Debbie said as she put on the apron. "My name is Deborah Ryans, but I go by Debbie. Deborah is too ostentatious. And Deb is an old wine aunt's name. Debbie is more fun."

"Yes, Debbie is fun." May said as she began scrubbing the shirt in the sink. "You look like a person who is very fun."

"Wow, thanks." Debbie said, although she was thrown off by May's tone. She wasn't sure if May's compliment was genuine or dismissive. "You look pretty um... well, you look pretty. That's true enough."

"Oh, thank you." May said, as she continued scrubbing. Debbie wasn't sure, but she thought May might be blushing once more. It was an encouraging sign, all things considered.

"Listen, May. I don't normally do this." Debbie swallowed, suddenly nervous.

"What do you mean? You don't normally do what?"

"Well, normally I take this kind of thing slow." Debbie said. "But I am only visiting in Europe. I don't have a lot of time to dance around. Sometimes it's better to just be upfront and honest about how one feels. I looked you in the eyes and you looked back at me. It was just a split second, but I really noticed something. So, I just thought I would ask-." The conversation was disrupted as the door to the backroom swung open. An older man burst in and began to berate May in gruff Romanian. Debbie could not understand what the man was saying, but she could read the subtext. The man was clearly May's boss, and he was upset at her performance. The man was rebuking May, and the young woman shrank under his verbal assault. Debbie felt the need to interject. "Listen Mister, don't be mean, she's a nice girl."

"Yes, sorry, you are not part of this." The older man said in broken English. He was clearly making a point of not looking in Debbie's direction. "This is not Maia's first accident. I am sorry." The man spoke a few more sentences to May in Romanian. The young girl was flustered, but she answered back in Romanian. Her reply was timid, and dejected. She had no fight in her. The man appeared satisfied. Abruptly he turned and left the back room.

"That guy was a jerk." Debbie said. "He wouldn't even look at me."

"Well, you're without a shirt." May said. "He didn't want to perv on your sports bra."

"Oh yeah, I forgot about that. What did he say?"

"He say I am fired. I spill drinks on you, and I spend too long back here. Also, I make other mistakes."

"What? Oh May, I'm sorry!"

"It's not big deal." May said. "I didn't really like this work anyways. I will just pack up and go home."

"Well, let me at least help you pack."

"You don't have to, it's not your fault."

"I know, but I want to." Debbie said. May turned from the sink to look Debbie in the eye. Once more the two women shared a moment of eye contact. A simple moment, but an intimate one. May still appeared shy and timid. But as she looked at Debbie there almost seemed to be a flicker of recognition in her eyes. A new understanding.

"Well, that might be nice. I have been very lonely lately. I wish to have a-." May hesitated for a moment, as though searching for the right words. "A new friend, perhaps? I will clear out my locker and then perhaps you can walk me to my home."

May handed Debbie back her shirt. It was still wet, but Debbie put it on anyways. She didn't care about the slight discomfort. She went back out to the front of the coffee shop, where Simon still waited for her. Simon was such a nice guy, a nice male friend. Debbie spoke to Simon sensibly. She told him she would be waiting for May. For one moment Simon looked slightly hurt, which confused Debbie. But it was only for a moment, then Simon excused himself and Debbie was free to wait for her new crush. It was an awkward wait, longer than Debbie had expected. The minutes ticked by like hours, first 10 minutes, then 20. She saw other people walking along outside of the shop, friends and couples together. Some looked her way, noting her as an outsider. Her foreign clothing, her unusually short hairdo, her Irish heritage. She stood out like a sore thumb. The people of the Romanian village didn't have to say a word. One look was enough to make Debbie feel like a stranger. Her relief was palpable as she saw May finally exit the coffee shop. "I thought I'd never see you again." Debbie kept her voice playful, but there was an element of truth to her statement.

"Yes, I am sorry." May said. "There were more details to finishing a job than I thought. I had to do some paperwork and hand in some things."

"Hey, you're worth the wait." Once more Debbie did her best to keep her tone teasing and playful. But once more there was more truth to her words than she wanted to admit. "What shall we do now?"

"Well, my home is with my parents in this town." May said. "It is perhaps twenty minutes' walk if you want to go with me."

"Sure, ok that's fine." Debbie said. "Have you been here a long time?"

"Yes, this is my home. I tried to leave to study but it was-." May paused for a moment, then her speech became more erratic. "I am sorry, I don't normally speak to people outside of work and my family. I say too much. I should just say I have been here most of my life."

"I'm pretty different." Debbie said. "My parents moved around America. Then they had me in Canada. It's a big country and we moved around a lot there. Then my dad had a job opportunity in Australia. So, they moved there while I stayed in Canada for University. Then I flew to Australia after I graduated. Now here I am, touring Europe to find myself. I don't really stay in one place too long."

"Wow, you must have seen many exciting things." May said. "I wish I could do things like that."

"Well, what's stopping you?" Debbie asked. "You're a free woman. You live in the western world. I don't know much about Romania, but surely women are as free here as they are anywhere else."

"Yes, that is true. But I sometimes cannot do things." Once more May hesitated as she spoke. "It is perhaps a problem with anxiety, yes? Normally I wouldn't be so free, talking about it. But I hope I can say it with you. I am sorry, I must sound foolish."

"No, I understand. Anxiety is normal and common." Debbie did her best to keep her words simple. May spoke English well, but she did seem to have some limits and Debbie wanted to be sensitive to those limits. "Perhaps it can be helped with a solid presence. Someone who is strong and stable. But also someone who is kind and sensitive to your needs. A warm and nurturing person, but also a firm foundation."

"I don't understand what you mean." May said. "Do you know someone like that?"

Debbie felt her heart sink at May's words. She had thought it was obvious she meant that she herself could fill that role. She had hoped May could pick up on her hints. But the young woman seemed confused. Debbie took a different approach. "May, I have a motorcycle. I am touring different parts of Europe to find new experiences. You know the area. Perhaps you could show me nice places to ride my bike."

"OK, yes I know some places." May's face brightened as she spoke. The idea of riding a motorcycle seemed to excite her, and her ability to offer advice seemed to invigorate her. They approached a house along a side street that May recognized. "This is my home. But please, let me have your cell phone. I can call and text. Give you information and meet you later." They exchanged information quickly, then May retreated back into the house. She was a shy young thing, but she had the means to contact Debbie again. Debbie supposed that would have to be enough. The young woman turned away from the small house and began walking back to the coffee shop. It had been a long walk, and the sun was low in the sky. Debbie still had to return to where she had parked her motorcycle.

As Debbie walked along the side streets of the small Romanian town, she felt the darkness of twilight envelope her. The sun had just dipped below the horizon. Though it was not yet nighttime, there were enough shadows for some denizens to hide. Debbie was young, strong, athletic, and confident. She had no reason to fear the shadows. So, when a disheveled man suddenly approached her in the darkness, she exhibited only a slight gasp of surprise. The man seized her forearm in a slight but firm grip. He spoke to her earnestly. "There might be danger for you, I'm not sure." Debbie began to wrench her arm out of the mysterious man's grasp. While she was an open-minded woman, it was unacceptable for a strange man to seize a lady no matter what the circumstance. Yet even as Debbie struggled under the man's grip, she happened to look into his eyes. Unbidden to her, a memory came flooding back to her mind.

***

Debbie's parents moved around a lot, meaning there weren't a lot of constants in her life. But one man that was consistent as she grew up was her great Uncle Adam. Uncle Adam, brother to her paternal grandfather and a veteran in the Gulf War. An anti-tank mine had detonated close to his head, rendering him clinically deaf and partially disabled. He had returned to Canada a simple man with an easy smile. He was slow, but in his own way he was honest and reliable. He was a man that Debbie's parents would trust to look after Debbie while they worked. Debbie's mother would often snark that Uncle Adam wasn't really taking care of little Debbie, instead, little Debbie took care of disabled Uncle Adam. Whatever the case, little Debbie and Uncle Adam spent a lot of time together in western Canada. Debbie remembered holding her great Uncle's worn and calloused hand as they would walk together in the Canadian wilderness.

The fact that Uncle Adam was deaf was a source of security for Debbie growing up. She could tell her great Uncle anything and he would keep it a secret. Her curiosities, her inner conflicts, her insecurities. She could be completely open to Uncle Adam, and he would never tell a soul. As a child, Debbie was a little chatterbox, and that worked out great for a deaf older man like Uncle Adam. She could tell him all manner of nonsense and it wouldn't matter. But one day, Debbie felt the need to tell her great uncle something a little more important.

They were walking along a provincial park path in British Columbia. Debbie had just reached her fourteenth birthday, and Uncle Adam was nearing his 70th. She held the old man's hand as the two walked along a path lined with pine trees, approaching a clearing that would reveal a fresh mountain brook. Why Debbie chose this moment to come out to someone, she would never know. But here, alone with her deaf great uncle Adam, suddenly Debbie wanted to announce something very important. "Uncle Adam, I love you and I trust you. So that's why I'm

11

telling you before anyone else. I know you're deaf and you can't hear me. But you're the first person in my life I'll say this to. So that's still something special." Debbie spoke the words, even though she knew her great uncle couldn't hear her. Just articulating them to someone she loved was important. "Uncle Adam, I'm gay." Just saying those words felt exhilarating, yet terrifying at the same time. "I'm gay. I'm a lesbian. Ever since I was little, I've known that I'm different. Growing up, every fantasy I've had involved another woman. Every desire I've had has been for women." Once more, Debbie felt conflicted saying these words. She was excited, yet her words felt like a taboo. Like she was breaking a rule saying them out loud. But she was alone with her deaf uncle, nobody could hear her. "It's the 21st century. I know there's nothing wrong with being a lesbian, but it's still terrifying saying it out loud. The same way a lot of things about growing up are scary but also normal. Like menstruation or acne, or body hair. I'm telling you this because I'm more comfortable telling it to you than anyone else." Debbie forced the words out of her mouth even as she saw her Uncle Adam looking away from her to the Canadian wilderness beyond them both.

Uncle Adam gestured to the stream they had walked along. He spoke with a voice that was slightly too loud to be socially acceptable. The voice of a deaf man. "Look Debbie! You can see trout jumping along the stream! They look so happy and full of life!"

Debbie couldn't help but laugh as she saw the fish leap up from the water. There were tears in her eyes, tears of happiness. "That's right, Uncle Adam, they look ever so happy." The young woman grabbed the older man in her arms and gave him a warm hug. Uncle Adam didn't fully understand the significance of that day, but he loved his great niece and he hugged her back with all of his heart.

***

The memory came back to Debbie in a heartbeat as she looked at the man now gripping her forearm. "Who are you?" Debbie asked.

"I go by GT, but my name doesn't really matter." The man said. He pushed something into Debbie's hand as he spoke. "What does matter is I have a feeling about you. You might meet something nasty soon. Something that doesn't die from normal means. If you meet something like that, shove this into its head or its heart."

Debbie shrank back from the man, still gripping the object in her hand. She looked down and saw it was a cylindrical object fashioned from sterling silver, sharpened to a point at one end like a stake. Normally Debbie would have never tolerated some random man accosting her in a dark alley. She would have refused to accept an object from such a man, possibly screamed and called for the police. But as the young woman looked into the eyes of this man, she found a feeling of warmth flow over her. He was dirty, scruffy, and he smelled funny. He looked like a homeless vagrant. But as Debbie looked into this man's eyes, she felt a feeling of trust and comfort. The same trust and comfort she associated with her Uncle Adam. She took the object from the man, reminding herself that his name had been GT. "OK, head or heart, you said?"

"Yes, stab its head or its heart." The man repeated the words, then rushed back down the alley between the houses of the small Romanian town. Debbie watched the man go, with a slight feeling of sadness. She looked down at her hands and saw she still held the silver stake in her grip. She slipped the object into her fanny pack, as she continued her walk back to the coffee shop. Her Kawasaki motorcycle was still parked out front. Debbie straddled the vehicle, revved the engine, and drove off into the night.

CHAPTER TWO

"What's this?" Debbie asked, as she turned the page. Taped to the corner of the scrapbook was a collection of pine needles.

"Oh, well, that's from our next time." May said, blushing. "Our first kiss. I took them from the trees near where you park your bike."

"That's right, I remember now." Debbie said.

***

At 5:30 am, Debbie's phone began playing Gotye's Easy Way Out. Debbie had set it as her alarm and the girl was a light sleeper. She sat up quickly in the hostel bed and turned off the music. The sun wasn't up yet, but Debbie wanted an early start to her day. She got out of bed, pulling on a tank top and sweatpants. She quietly went to the communal bathroom to brush her teeth. Then she walked down the steps of the hostel to the ground floor. It was the ground floor in Europe, not the first floor, one more little difference from North American terminology. But Debbie prided herself on being able to adapt quickly. She also prided herself on her good health, which she attributed to her habit of jogging every morning.

At least an hour of cardio every day, usually more. Debbie had run every day since she started running cross country in high school. In warmer weather, she could run anywhere. In the wintertime she went to a gym and ran on the treadmills. It was a simple, fun exercise, one that she could do alone. This early in the morning the streets were empty. Debbie could set her playlist and run until sunrise. She had a lot to think about.

Debbie's motorcycle had been making a funny noise when she had driven it home last night. She would have to ask the other members of her riding group about it. Debbie had found the online group "European Chopper Experiences" a few months ago. It had promised an all-expenses paid tour around the continent. Debbie had always wanted to travel, and she loved motorcycles. The movie "Easy Rider" had inspired her to experience both at once. But while Peter Fonda and Dennis Hopper had spent the entire film riding and camping alone, Debbie wasn't quite so bold. After all, the duo had died at the end of that film. She preferred a more structured tour with a group of people who knew something of the area. The internet made that group easy to find. The group was predominantly male. But having met someone new, perhaps that wasn't as much of an issue.

That was another thing Debbie thought about as she jogged: May's green eyes. Debbie had dreamed about May last night. It wasn't a particularly exciting dream, they had just walked and talked together. But in that dream May's voice had become too soft to hear, and all Debbie could do was look into those green eyes. As Debbie's feet pounded the pavement, she thought about how she should approach this. She had felt a connection with the young woman yesterday, and she was certain it was mutual. But May had been evasive. Debbie thought of a meme she had seen online about lesbian flirting being mistaken for friendship. The lesbian would tell a girl her butt looked amazing, and she wanted to get into her pants. The girl would respond: "Hey thanks, you can get these jeans at 'Old Navy' for an affordable price!" Debbie hoped her instincts were right about May's interest. But May had been difficult to read, and there was a cultural gap too.

Then there was that man that had bumped into her. Debbie didn't even know what to make of that encounter. In hindsight it seemed obvious that she should have just ignored the man, perhaps called the police if he'd hassled her. But there was something about him that spoke to her, even now. He had given her something, that detail also bothered Debbie. She was a young woman in good shape, naturally men offered her gifts on a pretty regular basis. Free drinks, free meals, one time in college a man had left flowers and a teddy bear outside of her dorm room. Another man had bought her jewelry. Debbie could read between the lines; she knew these gifts were romantic invitations. She would be polite, she would be friendly, but she would also be clear that she wasn't interested. She would refuse the gifts. The exception might be a drink or meal from a trusted male friend. In that case there was an understanding that since it was something small, she would pay it back somehow. That man GT had given her a chunk of silver that was still in her fanny pack back at the hostel. Debbie had no idea what to do with that.

As these thoughts went through her mind, Debbie saw the sun rising. She checked the time, to her surprise it was past 6:30. She had been running for over an hour. She felt her stomach rumbling. It was time for breakfast. Fortunately, the young woman had been jogging a circular path along the blocks of the town, so the way back wasn't that far. There was a sandwich shop on the same street as the hostel, a block down from the garage where ECE stored their motorcycles. Debbie was happy to see the shop was already open, and she took a moment to stretch before going in. She was surprised to see Simon already in the shop, he usually didn't get up this early.

"Debbie, top of the morning to you!" Simon said. "Let me buy you breakfast."

"Oh, hi Simon." Debbie reached into the pockets of her sweatpants and realized she had forgotten her wallet back at the hostel. "Actually, maybe I'll take you up on that. I know I owe you for yesterday, but I'll pay you back for both later."

"Hey, consider it a gift."

"No, I will pay you back." Debbie said, as she sat down across from her friend. The Romanian breakfast consisted of an egg, fried potato wedges, sausages, bread with zacusca, and a side of vegetables. Not that different from what Debbie was used to, but as with many European experiences, the little differences made it special. It was a filling meal, the perfect way for Debbie to finish her morning run. She ate in silence, which was fine, since Simon wanted to talk.

"Did you know Stanley Kubrick used special cameras and lenses from NASA for his filming techniques? It helped him film movies like Barry Lyndon using natural candlelight. He also made 2001 A Space Odyssey, a film so realistic it still holds up today. It's why a lot of people think he filmed a fake moon landing. The man was a master film maker. I often hear him compared to Alfred Hitchcock, but I've heard Hitchcock was a fraud. Like there's a rumour that he took the credit for the efforts of his wife, Alma Reville. Another example of men using a patriarchal society to exploit a woman's work."

Abruptly Simon stopped speaking. Debbie looked up from her meal to find the young man quietly looking at her. At once she had the impression of a dog waiting expectantly to be rewarded with a treat. Feeling at a loss, Debbie said the first thing that came to her mind. "So, you're interested in filmmaking? Ever thought of maybe doing it yourself?"

"Well yeah, I spent a year at film school. I dropped out, hoping to follow in Kevin Smith's footsteps and make my own movie. Technology has advanced to the point that a movie can be filmed cheaply and with minimal equipment. Sites like YouTube also allow indie creators to reach an audience without traditional distribution methods. I heard stories of Stephen Spielberg working on the movie Duel, how he went out into northern California and made a film in like 12 days. Then there was Don Coscarelli who did all those Phantasm movies. He once filmed a scene where he sat in the trunk of a car angling a camera up to an actor firing a shotgun filled with blanks. He got the shot he wanted, but at the cost of accidently lighting his face on fire. Then there was that film Easy Rider-."

"I like Easy Rider!" Debbie said. "I used to watch it with my friend Liz. It's one of my favourite films!"

"Yeah, totally cool." Simon said, pleased to see the eagerness on Debbie's face. "That's another movie that was part production, part road trip. In the scenes where they were sitting around the campfire getting stoned? The actors were actually getting high in real life."

"Sounds like a real adventure." Debbie said as she finished her meal. She stood up from the table. "Say, bit of a change of topic, but how well do you know bikes? Mine's been making kinda a funny noise."

"Well, I'm not an expert, but I'll take a listen if you like."

"Sure, how about I meet you at the garage in a few minutes. I just have to grab something from my room real quick." Debbie left the restaurant and jogged back to the hostel. She had to do a bit more than just grab something from her room. A quick shower was in order, and a change of clothes. Debbie smirked as she went through her travel bag. What followed next was no simple procedure. No, there was an art to how a lesbian dressed. It was one part practicality, one part comfort, one part defiant counterculture, and all summed up with a smug confidence that would allow a lesbian to pull off a fashion statement no straight girl would dare attempt. In choosing today's outfit, Debbie also had to keep in mind that she was about to work on her bike. She chose blue jeans with a sideways belt combined with a grey t-shirt and flannel vest. In colder weather Debbie might have worn a beanie, but for warmer summer months a red bandana was sufficient. It was simple and practical; with older clothes she didn't mind getting dirty. As the young woman walked out the door, she grabbed her fanny pack. She kept her wallet in there, and she was getting tired of being caught without money. Dressed for success, Debbie was ready to get to work.

The first thing she did upon entering the garage was push money into Simon's hands. The young man tried to protest, repeating once more he wanted to give her a gift, but Debbie wasn't hearing it. She had borrowed money, she was paying it back, and now they were square. Then Debbie knelt in front of her Kawasaki. It had been making a whining noise earlier, near the gas tank. She looked over the vehicle now but didn't see anything obvious. She looked for Simon, but he was at the other end of the garage. He had promised to help her, but now he wasn't even looking at her direction. Debbie felt a moment's frustration. Was Simon ignoring her because she had paid him back? She had told him from the start she didn't want him to give her anything. And he knew for a fact she was gay. Certainly, he couldn't think she was leading him on or being disrespectful. But why would he suddenly be avoiding her? Debbie stood from her bike as she watched Simon.

Simon was speaking to another member of ECE. The motorcycle group predominantly consisted of men, but apart from Debbie there was one other woman: Patricia Lyle. Demanding people refer to her as Trixie, the woman was a fat, middle aged biker from Iowa. A crass midwestern woman, with a foul mouth complimented by an easy cackling laugh. This mouth contained fewer teeth than normal. The absence of her front left incisor left a black hole for her breath to whistle through. Trixie embodied the stereotype of the loud boisterous American. The woman was coarse, the woman was loud, the woman swore like a sailor. Debbie was also convinced Trixie was secretly gay. Certainly, the older woman spoke often of men. In harsh terms she would speak of her ex-husband. In kinder terms she would mention her 21-year-old son who now lived in Nebraska. But though the older women spoke so often about men, Debbie was certain Trixie preferred women deep down. This general vibe made Debbie feel more comfortable around the older woman. There were other things to appreciate about Trixie as well. She was friendly and fun. She had a litany of dirty jokes and interesting stories to tell. Her easy laugh was contagious, and those around her found themselves laughing as well when they spoke to her.

Case in point, Simon was laughing right now. Trixie was saying something rather stereotypical about men's failure to perform sexually. And though such a comment might normally be offensive to men, Trixie was able to say it in a way that made Simon feel like he was in on the joke. Debbie had only heard part of the conversation; it concerned the size of male genitalia. But she heard Simon's reply quite clearly. "Oh yes, I am four inches. Four inches wide!" Abruptly Debbie saw Trixie stop laughing, a look of surprise on her face. It was subtle, and Simon probably didn't notice it. But even as Debbie watched, someone else entered the conversation: Gerard Whitman. Gerard was the organizer of ECE. He was an older man in his late 50s, tall, with long grey hair and a paunch of a stomach common to middle aged men. Gerard put his arm around Simon's shoulders, excusing himself and the younger man from Trixie. The two men went to another corner of the garage. They spoke quietly, but Debbie was still able to hear them.

"Listen Simon, this is important," Gerard said, "Never say dirty jokes around women. It's OK when they do it, but it's wrong when you do it. They could accuse you of sexual harassment."

"Sexual harassment?" Simon was taken aback. "But that would be a false accusation. I mean she joked about it first. It would be a lie."

"Women lie about that, kid. I learned that the hard way from my ex wife. Women can destroy your life if you're not careful."

"OK Gerard, you're right." Simon said.

Debbie felt her cheeks flush as she backed away from the two men. What a disgusting thing to say. Making those kinds of assumptions about women? It was a hurtful and sexist assumption from a man like Gerard. And watching Simon mindlessly agree with it was particularly chilling.

Debbie paused and took a deep breath. She prided herself on seeing both sides of important issues. If she wanted to be fair, it was true that sometimes women did lie about horrible things like sexual harassment. Lies like that ruined a man's life, and she wouldn't want something like that to hurt a friend like Simon. But how often did that really happen? It was pretty damn rare.

Debbie looked from the two men to Trixie. The older woman was still working on her own vehicle, a Ducati black and steel muscle bike. Was Trixie really the type of woman to lie like that? It was a hell of an assumption to make. Debbie walked forward. She was going to do what these men refused to do. She was going to ask Trixie what she thought.

As Debbie approached, the older woman rose and greeted her with a friendly gap-toothed smile. "Heya, hot stuff! How's it feel being the best-looking slice in this dump?"

Debbie giggled in spite of herself. It had been a crude remark, but complimentary nonetheless. "Hi Trixie, how are you today?"

"Well, I'm halfway to my grave, my ex-husband wants me dead, my son's abandoned me to live his own life, and it'd take a full bottle of whiskey to get a man into my bed. All things considered? This is way better than I thought I'd be doing at this age! How about you?"

"Oh, I'm- well, I'm fine." Debbie said. "In fact, I think I've met someone special."

"Oh yeah? Someone who doesn't need to shave in the morning, right? Nothing wrong with me saying that out loud, is there? You've been pretty open about your taste for the fuzzy stuff. Not that I'd judge one way or the other."

"Yes, that's right, I like girls. You know that." Debbie blushed as she spoke. She was open about her sexuality, but it was a challenge dealing with Trixie's blunt manner of speech. "But I kinda wanted to talk to you about something else. Just now, with Simon. The way you guys were talking. I think you said a sex joke and he said a sex joke back."

22

"Yeah, that happened, so what?"

"Well, it just-." Debbie searched for the right words. "You seemed a little upset. I'm wondering if it bothered you that a man said sex stuff, and if you think it's only OK when women make those kinds of jokes."

"What, are you kidding me? A joke's a joke." Trixie said. "It did kinda throw me that Simon would say something dirty back, but that's only because I always thought of him as being a shy guy. That he had the balls to say something nasty back, well I respect it, but I didn't expect it, if you know what I mean. I took a moment to adjust, that's all. But I don't care, it's a free country, he can say whatever he wants."

"So, it's not a double standard for you." Debbie said. "Simon and Gerard don't need to censor themselves to spare your feelings."

"Well, with Gerard, he's in charge of this group. We look to him for more of a supervisory role. With a guy like that, yeah, I maybe expect him to be held to some kind of standard. But Simon is just a regular guy, like us. He tells a joke, I tell a joke, whatever, we're all on the same level. A little guy like him, he ain't gonna shock me."

"OK, I think that makes sense. I understand how you feel." Debbie said. "Thanks for clarifying it for me."

"Hey, anytime. Us girls got to stick together." Once more Trixie let out a cackling laugh before turning back to her Ducati.

Debbie went back to her Kawasaki as she thought over what she'd just heard. Gerard and Simon had been wrong, at least in regards to Trixie. She wasn't about to claim sexual harassment for a minor comment, she wasn't that kind of woman. The men had just made unfair assumptions based on stereotypes. Debbie considered confronting both Gerard and Simon immediately. Going over their conversation again in her mind, it still upset her. But even as she thought about it, she began to think better of it. Perhaps it was OK for two men to have a private conversation. As unfair and sexist as it was, it was still just two men talking. Certainly, in her private moments, Debbie had made assumptions about men that were unfair as well. She wouldn't make a fuss, Debbie decided, she would just let it go.

With that decision made, Debbie revved her Kawasaki and tore out of the garage. Yes, her bike was making a funny noise, but it was still a functional and reliable vehicle. She could always find the source of the whine later. Right now, the young woman wanted to feel the wind in her hair. Even more, she wanted to feel the warmth of someone soft and beautiful. Debbie rode through the streets of the quiet Romanian town, following the same path she had taken the previous night, leading her to the door of a familiar house. The same house Debbie had dropped May off at the previous night. Debbie stood outside that house now, revving the engine of her motorcycle.

At a different time, under different circumstances, Debbie would never have dared to be so bold. She would have approached the small European house, bandana in hand, and knocked politely on the door. She would have begged whoever answered for a moment of May's time, and then respectfully asked May directly if she was free to spend time with her. But right now, with a head full of righteous fury, Debbie was a different person. Her frustration was expressed in the roar of her motorcycle engine. The neighborhood took notice as a middle-aged man emerged from the house. The man began speaking to her in a language she did not understand, presumably rebuking Debbie for the nuisance of intruding upon this quiet neighborhood. But none of that mattered. What did matter was the flurry of activity in an upper window of the house, the glimpse of May's face that vanished as quickly as it appeared. Even as that middle-aged man approached Debbie's bike, a young woman came out onto the street at an even greater speed. There was a moment of confusion as both Debbie and May argued in different languages with a man Debbie assumed was May's father. But this moment ended with Debbie riding off into the morning sun with May clinging to her waist on the bike behind her.

The two women drove for twenty minutes until they found themselves beyond the town limits. Then Debbie took an off ramp leading to a stop in the Romanian countryside. Flush from the recent excitement of their quick exit from town, the two women climbed off the bike. Debbie, exhilarated from her sudden departure from decorum, took a moment to stare into May's green eyes. She gently cupped the Romanian girl's cheeks in her hands, guided May's lips up, and kissed her full on the mouth. This was not normal for Debbie. Normally Debbie was a quiet, sweet, respectful person who would take time to get to know a girl and make absolutely sure she had permission before even holding hands. But at this moment, Debbie was in a different frame of mind. Something had gotten into her today, and it wasn't just her annoyance with the men at the garage.

Perhaps Debbie was inspired to change up her usual style due to being in a different country, on a vacation from her normal routine. Perhaps it was the sudden rush of plucking May from her obviously conservative household and tearing off like an outlaw rebel. Perhaps it was simply the free feeling one gets from riding a motorcycle at high speed in the clean country air of an early morning. Whatever the case, Debbie was feeling recklessly passionate, she wasn't in the mood to play things safe. Instead, today she was a woman of action. She broke the kiss for just a moment, stared deep into May's green eyes, and said something that she would normally never say. "You're sexy. I want you!" Simple words, but spoken with smoldering intensity. Even in the heat of the moment, Debbie half expected the girl to recoil from the blunt nature of this statement. Instead, May's response was to grab Debbie and pull her into a firmer kiss. So much for ambiguity, Debbie thought. When push came to shove, a girl like May appreciated assertive action.

As intense as the moment was, it ended as abruptly as it began. To Debbie's left, a strange sound floated to her ear. Thinking back, she couldn't quite describe it. It sounded partly like a human voice, but only if that voice was unable to articulate speech and was reduced to a screaming moan. At the same time, it sounded like sinew stretched beyond its threshold so that it slowly began to crack and break apart.

Mixed with these two competing sounds there was a buzzing tone emitted at a consistent high pitch. All of these elements combined to create an unsettling auditory experience that made the young woman's blood run cold. There wasn't much that Debbie would interrupt a passionate kiss for, but this did it. The two women broke apart abruptly as they looked at the source of the sound.

It looked like a giant worm with little wires sprouting out from it. The wires, perhaps six of them, reached out from the thick worm body and dug into the ground in front of it. They served the function of allowing the worm to pull itself forward as it wriggled its body for increased motion. These spindling limbs contorted and twisted in an unnatural way, reminiscent of a creature from a stop motion Tim Burton film. Most of the outside of the worm was dark green, though closer to the front it was a fleshy pink. In the center of this blotch of pink was a cavernous mouth lined with jagged teeth. The creature was perhaps a foot in diameter, and four feet long. It moved like a serpent, pulling itself across the forest with unnerving speed, despite relying on its spindly limbs for additional motion. The horrible sight of the creature, the disturbing sound it was emitting, and the impossibly fast and erratic pattern of movement it was exhibiting ignited a fresh rush of adrenaline in Debbie's body. When the creature pulled itself into a leap, the young woman had a split second to react.

With a hard shove, she pushed May out of immediate danger. Then without even thinking, she ran forward to intercept the creature's leap. Looking back, Debbie would never be able to explain what had gone through her mind. Perhaps a childhood of soccer practice was partly to blame, but the young woman reacted to the fast-moving object hurtling towards her by swinging her right leg and kicking it as hard as she could. Debbie's jogging routine had helped her build strong leg muscles, and the force of her kick reversed the momentum of the creature, sending it hurtling back away from the woman. The spindly limbs once more created inexplicable movement for the fiend, as they anchored it to the ground, halting the abomination's momentum and pulling it forward like an elastic band. Debbie let out a yelp as she dove out of the way. The woman's reflexes saved her from being pierced by the monster's jutting teeth. Instead, the creature slammed mouth first into the forest floor. It was up again in less than a second, angling itself for another leap. The creature didn't have eyes, its face seemed entirely composed of the giant mouth of crooked teeth. But this mouth was directed towards May, frozen in surprise on the ground where Debbie had pushed her. Once more Debbie had only a split second to act.

The young woman's flannel vest was thick material, and Debbie was able to shrug it off quickly. She gripped the flannel in her hands and pulled it over the mouth of the giant worm. While twisting the flannel over the sharp teeth, the young woman straddled the worm, attempting to pin the creature to the ground with her weight. The move did seem to disorient the creature, but it was stronger than Debbie had anticipated. The worm was smaller than her, but it bucked beneath her with a speed and violent strength that made her sick. She would have expected such force from a 2000 lbs. rodeo bull, not an overgrown worm with wires sticking out of it. The young woman managed to stay on top of the creature for roughly 10 seconds before being thrown onto the grass. She landed painfully on her fanny pack and felt something hard poke into her back. It was the silver stake GT had given her the previous night. As Debbie pulled the object from the fanny pack, she saw the worm continue to buck and twist in front of her. The flannel vest was still twisted around its mouth, and the monster appeared to be disoriented by this obstruction.

Debbie looked down at the long silver spike in her hands. It was solid and sharp, and she didn't know how long her vest would keep this strange violent creature confused. She looked over at May, still frozen in terror and huddled on the ground. That was the motivation Debbie needed. She was damned if she was going to let this disgusting thing near the frightened girl. With sudden fury, Debbie raised the silver stake and brought it down with a stabbing motion. The pure metal punctured the skin of the beast, and Debbie yelped as a sudden blinding blue light tore up from the injury. It looked like blue fire, but it wasn't hot. As Debbie pushed herself away from the twisted worm, the blue

fire spread from the silver stake, consuming the beast as it curled and lay still. Even as Debbie watched, the giant worm seemed to simply evaporate in the bright flame. It was gone in a matter of seconds, leaving the silver stake and the torn remains of her flannel vest. It was a mystifying experience, but Debbie shook it from her mind. She needed to make sure May was OK.

Debbie took the shy Romanian girl in her arms and held her as she shivered. "I don't- I don't know. I don't understand what happened. What was the thing?" May struggled to speak as Debbie held her close. "Everything was normal with you and me and suddenly it is there and now it is just vanishing." May paused for a moment, looking into Debbie's eyes silently. For just a moment they held each other close, then May spoke once more. "You are my hero, Debbie. I know that's in movies, but it's true now. You do dangerous thing to save me." May shivered, hugging Debbie tightly.

Debbie could feel the Romanian girl's ragged breath as they embraced. They were so close she could feel the vibrations of the girl's heartbeat against her own chest. It wasn't as passionate as their earlier kiss had been, but it was an intimate moment nevertheless. Debbie couldn't help but think of how intense this last hour had been. Normally her approach to meeting women was to send a message to an open lesbian through the internet. This was followed by long periods of conversation and flirtation. Often this ended with her being ghosted. But it had resulted with her experiencing two short term flings, and one more serious relationship that had lasted for over a year. Her usual approach to potential girlfriends was to be slow and cautious, but then gradually open up over a period of weeks or even months. Debbie had broken that pattern today.

It had been crazy. Even as she thought about it, Debbie found it hard to believe. First, she had roared up to the house of a girl she barely knew and carried her off like an outlaw. Then she had fought an impossible monster for May like a knight slaying a dragon. This was so not like her. But as these thoughts went through Debbie's mind, once more she looked down at the cute Romanian girl in her arms. With one finger Debbie lifted May's chin so the girl faced her, and once more the two women passionately kissed. Maybe slow and steady didn't always win the race when it came to courting women. Sometimes flames can ignite in no time at all.

CHAPTER THREE

"I'm honestly surprised how quickly our relationship developed."
Debbie said, as she looked down at the scrapbook. "I'm usually not one to kiss on the first date."

"Me neither." May said. "That is to say, not at all really."

"Am I your first?"

"No, not exactly." May said. "There was one more but it- I don't know how to say."

"Oh, it's fine, you don't have to tell me if you don't want to."

"No, I think is important I tell you." May hesitated. "But let me think of right way."

"Well in the meantime I want to see what else you collected." Debbie turned the page with her bandaged hand. This one opened to a picture of Debbie, May, and Trixie in the garage. "Oh, I remember this, Simon took this!"

***

The two women spent the rest of the day in the forest. The sun was setting when Debbie finally dropped May off at her parents' home. They had been gone for hours, but as they pulled up Debbie saw a stern older man was waiting for them. May would later explain his name was Mr. Andrei Popescu. As Debbie parked her bike, May hopped off the seat behind her and scurried into the house. Mr. Popescu watched her go, then turned to Debbie. "What do you think you are doing? You stay away from my little daughter. You don't have my permission to meet her."

"Are you kidding me?" Debbie had to force back a laugh. "She's like 23. We don't need your permission."

"I only tell you once, you stay away." The man turned from Debbie abruptly and stormed back into the house.

This would be one more way that Debbie's relationship with May would deviate from her normal behaviour. In her previous relationships, Debbie would treat her girlfriend's family members with the utmost respect, making a point to speak to them in an open and friendly way. Good communication sometimes helped more conservative parents understand that a lesbian relationship could be just as happy and fulfilling as any other relationship. But with May's father, Debbie changed her approach once again. If the man wanted to assume she was dangerous, Debbie felt a dark thrill in adopting that image. There was a certain appeal to sneaking behind a conservative father's back to help a lonely, sheltered girl embrace her wild side. It was a different role than Debbie was used to playing, but she quickly learned to enjoy it.

They met the very next day. Debbie had done her early jog, changed, then driven her bike to pick May up. May had told her father that she wanted to get a head start on finding a new job, that she would be handing applications out all day. Instead, the girls drove back to the garage together. Debbie was still concerned about the unusual sound her Kawasaki was making. Fixing her bike would be easier if she had a friendly face to keep her company.

"Simon hasn't come in yet. I was kinda hoping to introduce you to him. I've been trying to be his friend."

"Why try so hard?" May asked. "Do you like him?" Debbie frowned at the question. After the way they'd kissed one another, surely May wasn't still confused.

"Well, let me explain. There was this boy who had a crush on me back in university. His name was Justin Klein, he left flowers and a teddy bear outside of my door. It was a sweet gesture, but I don't even like that kind of stuff, and I don't accept gifts from boys anyways. So, I carried it back to his dorm room and knocked on the door. He wasn't in, so I just left it out front for him to take back. At the time it had seemed like the right thing to do, but looking back on it I should've been more subtle. Others in the dorm saw what happened and ridiculed him for suffering a public rejection. Also, he was shorter than me. Slim, and not very athletic. I wasn't completely out of the closet at that point, I was playing it safe. If anyone asked, I would just say that I was bi, but I think most people knew anyways. Regardless, this bizarre combination made people start a rumour that Justin wanted me to peg him."

"Peg, I don't understand. What is peg?" In response to May's question, Debbie pulled out her cell phone and searched the internet for images. She found a sketch of a woman with a toy strapped to her pelvis, about to penetrate a man's rear. She showed the image to May and the Romanian girl recoiled. "That is disgusting! What man would do so degenerate a thing?"

"What, that's really your attitude?" Debbie asked. "I mean, it's two consenting adults, they're not hurting anyone. I've done something similar with a woman."

"Yes, but he is a man. It is different with a man."

"How is it different?"

"It's disgusting. A man should act strong. Not become a woman. Men and women are different"

"May, you know I want to date you, right?" It was the first time Debbie had said it out loud, but a feeling of righteousness made her bold. She saw the younger woman nodding in response. "And I don't want people to judge us if we date. So, we should not judge others either. Doesn't that make sense?"

May paused for a moment. She seemed to be genuinely conflicted as she considered what Debbie had just said. "Yes, I guess you make sense."

Debbie sighed for a moment, then continued speaking. "Anyways, getting back to my story, people bullied Justin far more than he deserved. It was a weird rumour, but one that kept following him around. I guess they had a similar attitude to you: It was ok if I was a top, but it was shameful for Justin to be a bottom. He probably had other problems too, he was picked on a lot. He didn't drink and that made him stand out, as almost everyone else drank in their first year of uni. He dropped out after one semester. Looking back, I wonder how much of that was my fault, and if he's doing OK now. I mean all he ever did was try to buy me something kinda nice. Anyways, Simon seems kinda similar."

"He wants the peg too?" May asked.

"No I- I don't think so. That's not what I meant. Simon is short, interested in art stuff, not very athletic, but he seems friendly and generous. That's what reminds me of Justin." Debbie looked up as she saw the door to the garage open. Speak of the devil, Simon had just arrived, followed by Gerard. The two men had arrived together, apparently having just finished speaking, and each going to inspect their bikes. Debbie took May by the hand and lead her over. Simon's face brightened as the women approached. To Debbie's relief it seemed whatever had upset the young man the previous day was no longer bothering him. "Simon, I wanted you to meet my girlfriend, May." Out of the corner of her eye Debbie saw May blush at the word girlfriend, but she didn't deny it.

"Hi May, pleased to meet you." Simon held out his hand which May gently shook. "Are you a biker too?"

"No, I don't know how." May said. "But I want to try. I hope to learn from Debbie."

"I just wanted to fix that weird noise before I rode out again." Debbie said.

"Oh, is that still a problem?" Simon asked. "Hang on, we should get Gerard to look at it." Turning from the women, Simon called the older man over and all four of them inspected Debbie's Kawasaki. Debbie revved the engine and pointed to the gas tank as a short whine squealed.

"You don't need to worry about that." Gerard said. "That's just air escaping the vent in the gas cap. It's a small expansion and contraction that happens sometimes due to changes in heat around the area. You can just ignore it."

"Well, all's well that ends well." Simon said. "What's left on our tour anyways?"

"We have a tour planned around the Carpathian Mountains. As soon as Trixie and the other boys get in, we can head off."

"We're moving on to Hungary in four days, right? Will we get to see Count Dracula's castle before then?"

Gerard laughed. "You know that guy's not real, right?" Simon returned the laugh and the two men went back to their own bikes. May watched them go, then turned back to Debbie, suddenly anxious.

"Did he say you leave in four days?" May asked.

"Well, that was our plan." Debbie admitted. She hadn't thought of that until now. It was such a whirlwind of a relationship already. Things were happening so quickly. Now it was possible it would end just as quickly. "Look, I'm not just going to disappear. Let's enjoy our time together. I will think about what can be done." May still looked anxious, but she only nodded in reply.

It took another ten minutes for the rest of the group to come to the garage. Two taller men, Andre and Emmanuel, came in together. Andre was a tall, athletic Portuguese man. Emmanuel was also tall and muscular, half Haitian and half German. Emmanuel would joke he was a "Hai-Man," and that became Andre's nickname for him. Debbie had thought the nickname sounded rather culturally insensitive, but Emmanuel seemed to like it. The two men had met on the tour, but as they were both the same height, both in their late 20s, both spoke fluent English, and both shared the same interests, they had become fast friends. The two men looked over at Debbie and May as they entered and began laughing and snickering to themselves. Debbie couldn't hear what was said, but she felt her skin flush in anger. She did her best to ignore the men as she saw Trixie enter the garage. The older woman also looked over at Debbie and May, she also smiled. But it was a smile of delight as she walked over and offered May her hand.

"I'm Trixie. Nice to see another lady here. Been too much of a sausage fest." Trixie turned from the ladies before they could respond. She called out to Simon. "Hey WeeGee! You want to be a photographer dontcha? Get one of us girls." Debbie felt Trixie's broad arm drape around her shoulder as she saw Simon pull out his phone. She had a split second to smile before the flash dazzled her eyes. "Email a copy to each of us. One to me, one to Debbie, and one to... wait I didn't even get your name!" Trixie threw her head back in a cackling laugh. "Usually, it's the men who are too eager."

"I'm May." The young woman's voice barely rose above a whisper. It seemed Trixie's behaviour was overwhelming her. Debbie held May closer, trying to calm the shy girl with her presence.

"OK folks, don't want to interrupt, but I'm going to discuss today's route." Gerard said. There was a surety to his voice that commanded other's attention. The rest of the garage gathered around to listen.

Gerard Whitman founded ECE to fulfill a lifelong dream he had of endlessly biking around the globe. He was born in England but spent most of his young adult life touring the world through an enlistment in the Royal navy. He had retired after a few decades of service. This career had resulted in a reasonable pension, and a number of friends throughout Europe. Friendships forged in the military often lasted a lifetime, and though his friends spread out over multiple countries as the years went on, Gerard kept in contact with all of them. One day, the man woke up, realizing he was in his 50s with no family and no definite life goals. What he did have was a motorcycle and a network of friends throughout the continent. Some of these friends owned property, some of them owned businesses. A few phone calls, some paperwork, and Gerard came up with a simple idea. Rent from his friends at a regular time of year, with a discount earned from decades of friendship, and incorporate these savings into a motorcycle touring business. This would allow him to continue to travel, enjoy his love of motorcycling, and pursue a fun business endeavor with his old friends. Europe was a big place. Gerard could live his whole life and not see everything the landmass had to offer.

In regards to the actual schedule, Gerard liked to keep it consistent, but also allow for flexibility. Every day he would have something noteworthy planned for his clients, but if they wanted to go their own way for the day, he could relate. He would lead a daily ride in an area he wanted to see, the others could follow or split up as they saw fit. After all, they were adults. He just asked that they send him a text at the end of the night. That way he could be sure they'd gotten home safely. As Debbie mounted her bike and felt May's slender arms wrap tightly around her waist, she felt grateful for this freedom.

A ride into the Carpathian Mountains sounded wonderful, but she wanted to be alone with May. The two girls rode along with the rest of the group for the first leg of the mountain tour, then split onto an offshoot of the mountain highway. It was August, and the weather was warm, but the air felt cooler as the two girls ascended the mountain. Debbie kept her eyes open for points of interest and saw a stop that overlooked a wooded section of the mountain range. She parked her Kawasaki and the girls dismounted. Debbie took May's hand in hers and kissed her gently on the cheek. "Let's go for a walk."

The two women walked along the forested mountainside in silence. The sun was high in the sky, but the mountain air felt cool and crisp. Somewhere they could hear a bird chirping. May's small hand felt soft and warm in Debbie's grip, and she looked over at the Romanian girl with a smile. May was looking around the forest, she looked enchanted. "I've never seen this. It's so beautiful." The young woman said.

"This is pretty close to where you live. You've never come out here?"

"No, I have father that- he is- well, conservative. Strict too."

"Yeah, I noticed that." Debbie said. "What does your dad do, anyways? Is he like, a cop?"

"He is music teacher. And your father?"

"Well, my dad's a diesel mechanic. He's been working on heavy industrial machinery for most of his life. He is Canadian, but he got a juicy gig in small town Oklahoma for a while, that's where he met my mom. When he went back to Alberta, she went with him. That's where I was born, though I grew up in British Columbia. They went there for the weather, and for my great uncle Adam. Uncle Adam was getting on in age, he needed family close by to look after him. He died, but we grew to love the west coast. Then Dad got an opportunity to start a business with his friend in Australia. Mom and Dad went over there, but I stayed in Canada to study. Didn't actually go to see them until I graduated. I had something incredibly important to say to them and had to tell them face to face." Debbie checked herself. "Wow, listen to me rambling. I wanted to know more about you and ended up telling you half of my own life story in a single breath."

"I like to listen to you talk." May said. "It is soothing for me, for my anxiety."

"You suffer from anxiety a lot?"

"Yes I-." May paused, searching for the right words. "I don't know how to say exactly. I have good times, and I have bad times. On bad times I suffer and it hurts to leave a comfortable place like my house. But good times I can be happy. It helps to have someone fun by my side." May paused again. She looked Debbie in the eye and smiled shyly. "You are fun for me."

"Hey, you're pretty awesome yourself." Debbie said. She hoped the casual tone in her voice matched the rebel image she was trying to project to the timid girl. Inwardly, she was beaming with pride. So, May had problems and Debbie was the solution to those problems. That made Debbie feel special. Like a dashing hero sweeping a fair maiden off her feet. Sometimes people were just made to complement one another. It probably explained why their relationship seemed to be going so well despite having lasted such a short period of time. The two women were quiet for a while as they continued to walk hand in hand down the forested mountain path. It was a wonderful moment, and Debbie felt a surge of annoyance when the moment was abruptly interrupted

A grimy man, short and disheveled, was walking towards them holding a pump action 2 litre sprayer. Debbie tensed as the man spoke to them. She recognized the voice of GT, a man she had met once before. "Step aside." GT brushed passed the two women and began to spray vapour into the air a few meters passed them. As the two women watched in shocked amazement, the water vapour began to congeal into fat drops that splattered onto the ground.

"What- what is that? What are you doing?" Debbie asked.

"That is Parvulus Hirudo, a demon legion under Great Duke Astaroth. A swarm of tiny airborne parasites that consume human prey. They permeate your skin, sucking the blood from your veins to gestate into airborne swarms of larger demonic bugs known as Malae Turbela. What I am doing is spraying droplets of tap water over them. Instead of absorbing blood, they absorb the water. Then they swell up, drop harmlessly to the ground, lacking the necessary nutrients and protein strains to gestate and metamorphosize into their more advanced state. "

"What? I don't understand." Debbie stared at the grubby man in numb surprise.

"Well, the parasites are incredibly deadly because they so easily absorb on contact. If you touch them, they will consume you. But this easy absorption comes at a cost, because they will bond with tap water just as easily which will saturate and neutralize them. I don't know if I can explain it any better than that."

"Bro, I really don't know what you're talking about. I just wanted to spend time alone with my girl." Debbie said. This was a bizarre moment, and she was struggling to acclimate. "I remember you though, you gave me a weird present just out of the blue." It was starting to come back to her now, as she thought about it. She never normally accepted gifts from men. Especially men she didn't even know. But for some reason he had convinced her to take something really expensive. Like a big chunk of gold or silver. It was so unlike her to accept something like that, but looking back it was a good thing she had because otherwise she would never have... "Oh my God, I killed a giant monster with the silver thing you gave me!"

"That's right! I saw that!" Beside Debbie, May was gasping with equal surprise.

"How, how could I possibly have forgotten something like that?!" Debbie was starting to sweat as the memories flooded back to her. The gruesome giant worm with jagged teeth. She had kicked it like a soccer ball, then torn up her vest trying to restrain it. The memory had faded even as the demon had burned away in blue fire. Even now she struggled to recall specific details. The association with GT and his gift had been her link back to the memory. She felt genuine fear, and looked at GT. With his short greasy hair, his dirty skin, and weeks of stubble, he looked old. But as she looked closely, she could see he was a young man. And in his eyes, there was still that reassuring warmth and kindness. That same warmth that reminded her of her Uncle Adam.

"It's OK, I understand." GT said. Simple words, but for some reason they were enough. Debbie felt calmer now, safer. For a split second, she was tempted to hug the man.

"What is this?" Debbie asked. "What's happening to us?"

"It is the influence of the Great Demon Duke Astaroth and his minions." GT said. "A powerful demon affiliated with air and serpents. But perhaps his most deadly aspect is his ability to control and influence the human mind. I fought one of his peers before, Duke Vepar. Vepar's power was to infect victims with wormy parasitic infections that would quickly kill and consume them. Astaroth is more subtle. Instead of killing people who pose a threat to him, Astaroth simply changes the way people think. Any memories of him or his legions are quickly forgotten. Your thoughts become rationalizations and dismissive justifications. Instead of fighting him you shift your attention to playing with friends or flirting with potential lovers. Or maybe something else, like pursuing some hobby you always had an interest in. Anything to distract you from the looming sword of Damocles that is slowly readying to strike. It is a constant influence, so long as the demon is present on Earth."

"Wait, you mean this will happen again?" Debbie asked. "My memories will fade again?"

"Yes, they might come back if something triggers them, like an obvious encounter with another demon. Or maybe if you speak to me again. But they'll constantly fade from your mind. For the most part you'll continue to live your lives oblivious of any danger. That is how these demons keep you vulnerable, constantly exposed to the element of surprise."

"Oh God, this is horrible!" Debbie cried out as she felt May shiver in fear beside her. "You're telling me demons are going to take over and we won't even remember it's happening?"

"I'm going to take care of it." GT said. A simple sentence, but a powerful one. Debbie suddenly found herself thinking of an early childhood memory, when she was four years old and scared of the boogieman. Her father had promised her he would beat up the boogieman, and she would never have to worry about him again. The love and trust she had felt for her father at that moment, she felt the same emotions now looking into GT's eyes.

"Thank you." Debbie said, she struggled to blink back tears. "What can I do if I see another monster myself?"

"Well, you still have the silver I gave you." Gently GT took Debbie's hand, she saw he had a pen in his other hand. He wrote words on the skin of her arm: Salt, lighter, water, weapons. "Different demons have specific weaknesses. Some are vulnerable to salt, some to fire. You already saw me using water to neutralize the legion that was going to attack you. And some can be hurt by normal weapons like guns or knives. Hopefully if I write that down for you, you can remember to keep those items close. They'll make you significantly more combat effective." GT stepped back, and his kind eyes swept from Debbie to May. He shook his head gently, seemingly from amusement. "Romans 1:26." GT said, though this statement seemed to be directed to himself. He turned from the women and walked back into the forest.

"Romans 1:26?" Debbie asked groggily. She felt as though she was waking up from a dream. "Why did that man say that to me?"

"I don't know." May said. "I think it is from the Bible."

Debbie took out her cell phone and did a search. The mountains did not provide the best connection to the internet, but she did get a result back. Romans 1:26: 'Because of this, God gave them over to shameful lusts. Even their women exchanged natural sexual relations for unnatural ones.' As Debbie read, she saw articles explain that this passage was considered one of the clearest condemnations of lesbianism in the Bible. Debbie felt her face flush with anger. The man she had just talked to, she had been confused, but she had thought he was a friend. But here he was quoting the Bible, denouncing her as a sinner for the way she was born. Debbie fought to suppress her rage. It wasn't the first time she'd dealt with bigotry, but nothing enraged her more than being betrayed by someone she had considered a friend. She turned back to May, forcing herself to smile. "This has been a nice walk, but how about we head back to town. I'll buy you dinner." May nodded and the two girls walked back to the Kawasaki.

CHAPTER FOUR

Turning the page of the scrap book, Debbie saw a medical bracelet taped to the next segment. "Oh my God, you kept that?!"

"I collected every moment." May said. "The good and the bad."

"This one isn't good or bad." Debbie said. "It's just embarrassing."

***

Gotye's 'Easy Way Out' jerked Debbie from her sleep. It had been a vivid dream, epitomized by a solitary image of a man in gold surrounded by a shadowy wreath whispering darkness in his ears. Other details of the dream were quickly fading from her memory, but that one image still stayed with her. A golden man, haunted by a wispy shadow. Debbie did her best to shake the image from her mind as she pulled on her sweatpants. It was time for her morning run.

Debbie grinned with satisfaction as her feet propelled her across the pavement at a steady pace. She would breathe in through the nose, out through the mouth. Keep the pace with her arms. She remembered her high school coach had told her that her arms are closer to her head, so they were smarter than her legs. Keep a rhythm with her arms and her feet would follow. She pushed herself forward, her athletic body gliding across the sidewalk. Already her stomach was rumbling with hunger, but that was just part of the routine. She had to earn her breakfast with the effort of this run. Only after she'd put the work in to keep herself healthy would she allow herself to fill her belly. She circled the same blocks several times, a regular section of pavement with little incline. She jogged at a constant pace for 45 minutes straight. Then she slowed her pace for another 15 minutes and ended with some stretches. Her morning exercise complete, she stopped at the sandwich shop across from the garage. Once more she saw Simon getting his breakfast. It seemed he was making a habit of getting up earlier now, so her morning routine was starting to line up with his.

"Hi Debbie, let me buy you breakfast."

"That's sweet, Simon, but I remembered my wallet this time. Why don't you get us a table and we'll eat together." Simon prepared them a table in the corner as Debbie secured another breakfast of eggs, fried potato wedges, sausages, bread with zacusca, and a side of vegetables. It had filled her up the last time, so Debbie decided to stick with what worked. She sat across from her friend, breathing out a sigh of exertion. "I feel kinda weird this morning. Think it's because I had an off encounter yesterday. Met this weird scruffy mountain man. Don't even remember much about it except he quoted this anti lesbian Bible passage to me."

"Yeah, the Bible has been used to suppress the rights of women and particularly the sexual freedom of lesbians. It is only through the efforts of prominent lesbian feminists like Sarah Lucia Hoagland that women have been able to break away from the slavish chains of the patriarchy and embrace lesbian separatism from men."

Debbie looked up from her breakfast to see Simon beaming at her. Once more she had this odd feeling like Simon expected to be rewarded in some way for what he'd just said. "I just meant that it hurt my feelings. I remember thinking of this man as a friend, and it felt like a let-down that he was judging me for my sexuality. It felt like a betrayal."

"Yeah, sometimes it can feel like all men want to keep you down. I read about that, how the patriarchy is used to keep women oppressed and to this day results in women making 77 cents for every dollar a man makes. But I want to be a good ally, and fight for your rights."

"That has nothing to do with what I just said." Once more Debbie saw Simon leaning towards her with an expectant look on his face. She felt a new flush of irritation as another realization dawned on her. "I really gotta ask, Simon. All this feminist stuff, do you actually care about that at all? Do you seriously give a single crap?"

"Well, everyone should care, right?"

"That's not what I asked, Simon. I asked if you personally care about this stuff. Because I don't care about it at all, and I get the feeling you're just saying it because you think it's what I want to hear."

"I- Debbie, I do want you to like me. I want to be important to you, I want to fight for you."

"I don't like talking about politics, Simon. It's understandable that you might make this assumption, but just because I'm a lesbian doesn't mean I'm obsessed with feminist issues. Please don't buy into that stereotype. Just talk to me like a normal person. Be honest and open and don't try so hard to please the women around you."

"Well, OK, I guess I do try too hard and overthink things. That's always been a problem for me." Simon looked down at his own breakfast as his tone began to change. "I remember this one time, I had a roommate who had his girlfriend over all the time, and that girlfriend had a female friend who would come by. The girlfriend was named Laura and her friend was named Sandy. There was this time while Laura was talking to my roommate that I socialized with Sandy, and she abruptly got really weird and left as I tried to talk to her. For weeks I thought I'd creeped her out. Eventually Laura explained to me that it had nothing to do with me at all. Sandy had her period early and she left me because her pants were soaking through with blood."

"Oh my God!" Debbie choked out her sausage, caught halfway between amusement and disgust. "I walked right into that one, didn't I? I told you directly to be more honest, so I have no one to blame but myself."

"What? I thought you'd find that story relatable." Simon looked distressed. "I thought girls didn't get grossed out when hearing about periods and menstrual stuff."

"Hearing a guy talk about it is weird, OK?" Debbie took a deep breath, she was finally confident she wouldn't choke on any of her food. "I guess I can't really micromanage how you do conversations. Best I can say is you need to be honest and genuine, but also keep it light. Don't talk about religion, or politics, and particularly when speaking to girls avoid talking about sex. I don't just mean having sex. I mean anything graphic about sexuality or anything about men and women's parts. Like don't say anything about periods or testicles or anything. Try to find something kinda safe and interesting that the other person will also like. For example, you like movies, try talking more about movies you like."

Debbie's advice had been hard for Simon to hear, but as he listened to her talk, the words made sense in his mind. Taking a que from her, Simon thought for a moment, then began an explanation of Fritz Lang's contributions to the art of German Expressionism. He went on to mention how it had influenced the Red Hot Chili Peppers' music video for their hit song "Otherside." It was a fun, animated conversation, and it saw them through the rest of their meal. With the brief awkwardness behind them, Debbie and Simon walked together to the biker garage.

Simon went to say good morning to Trixie as Debbie went to inspect her Kawasaki. Going over her bike was routine now, an easy mindless task. She could do it and also notice Hai-man and Andre come into the garage. She probably appeared more focused than she actually was, which might explain why the two men felt comfortable looking at her and laughing to one another.

"She got herself a squeeze already. You gotta give it to her. She has more game than us." Hai-man said. "Course, it probably doesn't really count in her case. I mean, gays don't usually have to work hard for tail."

"Think their periods have synched up yet?" Andre asked with a laugh.

Debbie felt her face flush as she continued to go over her bike. She knew that was generally how guys talked, and they didn't really mean anything by it. In fact, she had heard far worse. But at the same time what they were saying was still sexist and disrespectful. She didn't want to be a killjoy, but she also didn't want to tolerate bigotry. She wondered if it was better to confront the men, or just ignore them. Fortunately, Trixie came to her rescue.

"You boys are confused about periods?" Trixie called out. "Doesn't surprise me one bit. You fellas look pretty inexperienced. What would you know about a woman's privates?"

"Now Trixie, that's not ladylike." Andre's tone was playful.

"How about I yank your pecker out till it's 3 feet long, wrap it around your buddy's neck and start him like a lawnmower, how's that for ladylike?" Trixie responded.

The two men stared at the older woman in silence for a moment, completely bewildered by the absurd statement. Then they looked at one another and collapsed in a cacophony of high-pitched giggles. Debbie shifted her attention back to her bike, satisfied. Trixie had done her job for her. And Debbie's Kawasaki was looking good. She had just finished her inspection when she saw Gerard standing in front of her.

"Everything in order?" Gerard asked. Debbie nodded as the old man continued. "That's good. I just wanted to talk to you about yesterday. You didn't text me at the end of the night."

"Oh, that's right. Sorry about that."

"It's not a big deal." The old man continued. "Just try not to forget in the future. Part of the business, I have to make sure everyone is safe."

"Hey Gerard, can you take a look at this? I don't know what's wrong with my bike." Simon called out from across the garage. As Debbie watched, Gerard went up to Simon's bike and immediately identified the problem. When it came to bikes, Gerard knew his stuff. The old man never seemed confused, he never hesitated. No matter what the mechanical issue, he was able to immediately identify the problem and offer a solution. Debbie's father was the same way. It seemed like magic watching men like that work. How quickly and easily they were able to rectify an issue that mystified Debbie. Of course, the young woman knew it wasn't really magic. It was years of experience, earned through a career of hard work. Debbie hoped one day to have that knowledge herself. Although she was a university graduate, she found her interest gravitated more towards blue collar careers. Working in the trades, rolling up her sleeves and getting her hands dirty. A lesbian stereotype, perhaps, but it was something her father did as well. There was nothing wrong with a girl following in her father's footsteps.

Debbie's train of thought was interrupted as she saw May walk into the garage. Debbie watched May walk by Hai-man and Andre. The two men smiled at the young Romanian woman, greeting her respectfully. They weren't laughing now; they weren't making off colour jokes. Debbie wondered why the men chose this moment to be on their best behaviour. She looked over at Gerard, still helping Simon with his bike. The presence of an older male authority figure probably had an impact. Gerard had a business to run, and he discouraged anything that could be considered harassment. But Debbie wondered if there was more to it than that. May was a meek and submissive looking girl. She wore makeup and feminine clothing. Unlike Debbie and Trixie, May looked more like a conventionally attractive girl. The type of girl that the men would consider dating. Once more Debbie felt a moment of anger and frustration. The boys weren't really doing anything wrong this time, and there wasn't really anything Debbie could do. But it still felt unfair. She shook the thought from her mind and revved her Kawasaki. She was going to take May for a ride.

The two women tore out of the garage and drove east of the town. They had gone into the mountains before. This time Debbie wanted to share a different experience with May: A walk amongst the Romanian farmlands. Eastern Europe had a lot of a beautiful areas to explore. As Debbie watched the road fly by beneath her motorcycle, she saw the simple agrarian countryside and thought of fairy tales she'd been told as a little girl. The world was always changing, but history was preserved in Europe more than almost anywhere else in the world. The farms the two girls drove by didn't look that much more modern than those that had existed for a hundred years or more.

Debbie pulled her bike over at a farm with a large sign that read "Dalca" in bold letters. She saw a large barn, and next to it a store open to the public. Some form of tourist trap certainly, but it was still something unique and interesting. The two women went into the store, and Debbie was happy to support a local business. Consuming an early lunch, they went to the outside of the barn and saw cows standing at its entrance. They were docile creatures, chewing contentedly on their cuds. But just seeing these animals was a novelty for both girls. A novelty for Debbie because she was new to the Romanian countryside. A novelty for May because she tended to stay in her hometown. Both girls loved animals.

"I am glad to share this with you." May said. "I am often scared of the idea to get involved with a woman. People judge. But you are worth it. Normally it would be easier to be with a man."

Debbie wondered at this statement. Did this mean May was bisexual? Or was she a lesbian so closeted that she dated men she had no interest in? It was still early in their relationship, so she didn't want to interrogate May too much. She didn't want to judge either way. She had had her own difficulties coming out. Debbie chose her words carefully. "We all come to understand ourselves in our own time."

"Tell me about you. You have many women?" May reached her hand out and gently stroked the snout of one of the cows. "Tell me about how it is in Canada. It is freer there, right? You must have many dates. Tell me about your experiences."

Debbie hesitated as she considered the question. There was a vibrant gay community at her university, and she had enjoyed positive experiences. But she didn't think May actually wanted to hear about her sleeping with other women. The two girls walked away from the barn as Debbie considered what she wanted to share. If May wanted to hear about her experiences in the west, Debbie could paint a picture for her. "Well, there's one experience that comes to mind. Let's go for a walk and I'll tell you."

It had happened four years ago. Debbie had already told May how her father had taken over a partnership in a mechanic garage in Australia. It was excellent money and he had dropped everything and crossed the Pacific with her mother. Debbie had stayed behind in Canada, studying Psychology at UBC. A useless degree, but it was what her generation did. They all studied useless subjects in university to put off the truth that entry into any gainful white-collar career was almost impossible. It had been an easy transition, as some of her friends from high school were going to the same university. Entering their first year of university, they were all 18. That made them 1 year shy of the legal drinking age. Together they would look for bars that wouldn't card.

Drinking age in Canada was 19. Getting away with underage drinking had been so much more fun. Cookies stolen from the jar tasted far sweeter than those taken with permission. Debbie had found gay clubs tended to be laxer in checking IDs than other establishments. So, she found herself in a gay bar called 'Strikers.' It catered more to men, but as bars catering specifically to lesbian women were relatively sparse in Vancouver, a significant number of queer women graced the establishment as well. It was an interesting experience coming to that bar. She had shown up one day, acting like she had belonged there. She had been friendly with the staff and behaved herself. She came back every weekend until the staff recognized her. She had never shown them her ID, but they felt familiar enough with her that they must have assumed she belonged there. That gave her free reign to consume drinks, then burn those calories on the dance floor. Debbie was a terrible dancer, but in a dark club with strobe lighting, nobody could tell. And Debbie didn't care, she would just close her eyes and move to the beat.

Her eyes flew open as she felt an invasive hand rubbing along her lower stomach. A low, feminine voice whispered in her ear, "You're looking sexy tonight, aren't you?" Debbie pulled herself away and turned to see an overweight woman leering at her. Abruptly Debbie had walked off the dance floor, heading to the washrooms in the back of the establishment. She felt her skin crawl as she moved, cringing as she relived the sensation of that invasive hand groping her. The hand had only rubbed along her stomach, but it was still a hideous experience. In the lady's restroom the music of the club was subdued, and Debbie splashed water on her face. She was still fairly drunk, but the encounter had rattled her. As she looked up from the sink, she saw the door to the restroom open and the same overweight woman entered the washroom.

"You shouldn't have run off after sharing that tender moment with me."

"Who are you?" Debbie asked. She still felt disgusted and violated. In hindsight she might have preferred to say something more dismissive. But at that moment it was all she could think of.

"I'm Ashley. I'm gay, I can tell you're gay. I've been watching you and I like what I see. We're all alone in this washroom. Perfect opportunity."

"Opportunity for what?"

"Don't be coy. I just said I'm gay, you're clearly gay. We're both women."

"No, you're not my type." That was all that Debbie was able to say. She was still thrown off balance, this situation felt surreal.

"What, I'm not good enough for you?" Ashley demanded angrily. "What's wrong with me?"

"I don't even know you." Debbie said. "Just because I'm gay doesn't mean I'm automatically going to have sex with you."

"I'm offering my body to you. What are you judging me for being fat?" Ashley looked genuinely hurt now, which Debbie found bewildering.

"I said no." Debbie felt her anger rising now. That was good, anger gave her courage and made her more assertive. "What's wrong with you, anyways? Do you think consent is only for straight people? 'No means no' isn't just for boys, it's for everyone! I don't owe you my body. Why are you perpetuating rape culture?"

Upon hearing the word 'rape,' Ashley recoiled in shock. It seemed Debbie's words had finally gotten through to the larger woman, as suddenly she began to break out in tears. For a moment Debbie felt the need to take the large woman in her arms, comfort her and tell her it was OK. That was her instinct whenever she saw someone crying. But in this circumstance, she felt it was better to keep her distance. "I'm sorry, I didn't mean it like that." Ashley said. "I just thought if I took the initiative, it'd turn you on. I'm not that good at this."

Recalling the memory still made Debbie shudder slightly as she finished telling the story to May. "We decided to just be friends. And in a few weeks, she hooked up with another girl that liked her. I still remember how invasive it had felt. It was awful the way she'd groped me from behind, without even knowing me. Some things just stay with you. But it ended well enough, so I try to just let it go."

"She didn't have consent." May said.

"No, she certainly didn't."

"But you do." May said.

"Yeah, I make a point of always respecting that." Debbie said. "It's the right thing to do."

"No, I mean right now." May said. "I have thought about it and I tell you that you have my consent. I buy toys and I want to have experience with you now."

For a moment, Debbie was taken aback. She hadn't expected such an abrupt invitation from the submissive young woman. But as she looked down at May's beautiful green eyes, she felt her heart beat a little faster in excitement and anticipation. They had been walking along the highway, and just off the road she saw an older barn. It looked abandoned and unused. The type of building two young woman could sneak into and enjoy an afternoon of privacy.

It was two hours later when the women entered the emergency ward of the hospital. The hospital waiting area was blessedly empty as Debbie led May by the hand towards the front desk. Both women felt mortified, but Debbie had always believed in putting one's health foremost. Even as they approached the administration desk, Debbie cringed again as they saw the older woman seated behind it. Said woman looked proper and stern, and at the sight of her May shrank back and buried her face in Debbie's shoulder. That was fine, Debbie thought, she would take charge. "Do you speak English?"

"Yes." The older nurse spoke with a heavy Romanian accent.

"OK, well. This is my-." Debbie hesitated. "May is my girlfriend. We were intimate today and I inserted a toy into her-." Once more Debbie paused as she struggled with the words. No, as embarrassing as this was, she would endure it for May. Debbie spoke again, forcing the words out. "I inserted a toy into her- into her rectum. And now we can't get it out. We need help, please."

Debbie expected the older woman to recoil in shock. Or for the woman to respond with stern admonishment. Instead, the nurse spoke with a sympathetic and professional tone. "Understand. I have form for you to fill out, doctor will be free soon. It is not busy tonight." Debbie took a clipboard from the nurse and she and May began to fill it out. May was still mortified, but she was comfortable talking to Debbie. Together they were able to establish the young woman's medical history and complete the form. Within ten minutes they were escorted to a private room where they were greeted by a young doctor in his early 30s who introduced himself as Doctor Fischer. He initially offered to speak to May privately, but the young woman insisted Debbie remain by her side, holding her hand tightly. May wanted Debbie to understand what was going on, and she didn't want to be alone.

"That is fine." Doctor Fischer said. "I know it is the 21st century. Lesbian relationships are understandable. Now, please tell me what happened. The more information you give me, the better I can treat you."

"We were fooling around and I was using a small vibrating silicon toy to-." Once more Debbie had to force the words out. Dr. Fischer seemed like a kind and understanding person, but this was still an awkward subject to talk about. It was even harder going over it with a man, but he was a doctor, and this was a medical issue. "I was using it to pleasure her. And in the heat of the moment, I slipped it into her bum to give her additional stimulation. It was stupid and we lost it up there."

"Completely understandable." The doctor said. "Can you describe this toy in more detail please?"

"Well as I said, it's made of silicon. Maybe 3 inches in length, half an inch in diameter. It has a button on it to change vibration modes. I was able to use my finger to press that button to turn it off. But when I tried to fish it out it just slid deeper into her."

"OK, I understand." The doctor said. "So, it's an object that's actually designed for insertion. That by itself makes you ladies smarter than some people."

Debbie felt herself relax a little at the doctor's words. "So, this isn't too crazy then?"

"Professionally speaking I can't comment about anything specifically. What I hear from my patients remains confidential. Just as you can be assured what you tell me tonight is confidential. But I will say that in general there are many people who get curious and experiment with many odd things. They often lie about what happened, making it harder to treat them. The fact that you ladies had the courage to speak to me honestly makes it much easier to help you."

"Well, what can we do to help May? Will she need surgery?" At the mention of surgery May squirmed uncomfortably and Debbie felt the girl's grip tighten on her hand.

"That is an option, as a last resort. But it's probably not necessary. For now, I think we should give May some time. She might just excrete the object out naturally in the next few hours. If that fails, we will perform an endoscopy to ascertain the exact nature of the blockage. We may perform a laparoscopy for surgical removal. But as I said, that procedure might not be necessary. What I want you to know is, one way or the other we will get it out and May will be just fine."

"Thank you doctor." Debbie said. "I just feel so ashamed. This is all my fault."

"Think of it this way. When a man eats lots of sugar and doesn't brush his teeth, it's his fault that he gets a cavity. Yet nobody shames him when he goes to the dentist. So why should other medical problems be treated any differently?" The doctor's words comforted the two women, and the apprehension they had felt in coming to the hospital relaxed.

"Your English is excellent." Debbie said.

"Thank you, I studied at Barts." The doctor said

"Barts, what's that?" Debbie asked.

"Oh, it's the common name for Saint Bartholomew's Hospital Medical College. It's the oldest in the United Kingdom."

"Who is Saint Bartholomew?" May asked.

"I believe, he is the patron saint of medicine." The doctor said. "If memory serves me, the association comes from ancient paintings and statues of him. They show detailed and fairly accurate depictions of the human muscular system, at a time when such anatomy was not commonly displayed."

"I don't understand." Debbie said. "Why would paintings of him show muscles like that?"

The doctor seemed to hesitate for a moment. "I'm sorry, perhaps I am getting off track. It is best we focus on the current medical situation. Let me just say again that one way or another, we will help you be well."

Time passed. The doctor checked on them periodically while May lay on the hospital bed. After a few hours, Debbie excused herself to find something to drink. Walking down the hallways of the hospital, Debbie was surprised to bump into a familiar figure. A dirty man dressed in torn clothing. Debbie watched as the man grabbed some bandages from a medical closet and began to dress a cut on his arm.

"GT, we meet again." Debbie said. Then she thought of their last encounter. The memory was hazy, but one detail stood out. "You mentioned Romans 1:26."

"I did." GT said, continuing to dress his arm. His injury had been bleeding, but the bandages stemmed the flow of the blood.

"How could you say that?" Debbie suddenly felt her face flush with anger. "I know what that means. It's a passage in the Bible that condemns lesbians. I thought you were a nice guy. How could you judge me like that? I feel really hurt and betrayed. You know traitors go to the lowest circle of Hell, don't you?"

"That's Dante's Inferno." GT said. "I don't consider that valid religious canon." Debbie had nothing to say in response to this statement. She could only stare in mute disbelief. Seeing this, GT spoke again. "OK, I see that I upset you. I apologize."

"You think I'm a sinner?" Debbie asked.

"Well, we are all sinners, everyone without exception."

"Dammit GT, you're missing the point again! Do you think I'm going to Hell just for the way I'm born?"

"I don't know. I've been taught only God can judge that. But I wonder if God is real, or if there are angels or Heaven. I know there is a Hell, but that's all I've seen."

"So, you mentioned Romans 1:26 because I'm going to Hell?"

"No, I mentioned it because of how ambiguous it is. All the teachings I've read center around men. The Bible speaks at length about men in all things. Male sexuality is outlined in great length. Passages like Leviticus 18:22 expressly forbid male homosexuality. But religious texts are not nearly as forthcoming in regards to women. In the Bible, women tend to only be mentioned as they relate to men. For example, Mary's most notable quality is that she is the mother of Christ. Sarai is only mentioned as the wife of Abraham. Some scholars could point to Ruth and Naomi, but I see that as more of a mother and daughter relationship. In that story Ruth ends up married to Boaz, so even she is defined as a man's wife. As religious texts focus on men, very little thought is given to how women act independently of these kinds of roles. And demons often exist as an inversion of the Holy Word of God."

"I don't understand what you're saying." Debbie said. "What does all of this have to do with Romans 1:26."

"Romans 1:26 is the closest the Bible gets to talking about lesbians, and even that passage is vague. It just describes unnatural acts, which could be interpreted as anything. And as I recall, in that passage only the men are specifically punished for sex, not the women. I figured since so little thought is given to lesbian women by both scripture and demon lore, that lesbians could be a blind spot. A gap in the knowledge demons possess when dealing with humanity. You could be something that the forces of Hell are not prepared for. I had a female ally once before, but she was straight. Demons often have the power to make women love men and my previous partner was coerced by a demon's influence. She was seduced by her love of men, and it really hurt her. When I mentioned Romans 1:26, I did so hopefully. I thought a lesbian woman might be a significant ally against the forces of Hell. That you might be immune to the traditional demon influences over men and heterosexual women. But I realize I was assuming too much. You don't even seem to notice my injury. Clearly you are as docile as anyone else. That's OK, it's not your cross to bear." GT spoke these words robotically, keeping eye contact with Debbie and blinking infrequently. It was a lot of information to take in.

"No, I noticed the injury. I just didn't know if I should mention it. It didn't look that serious. How did you get hurt?"

"An Inanis Campe."

"What's that?"

"Also called the Vain Wind." GT's tone remained level as he began to elaborate. He spoke without inflection, listing details in a matter-of-fact way. "It's a collection of small mothlike demons with razor sharp wings. They manifest on earth in a swarm of thirty-five and seem to operate with a single consciousness. I was able to dispatch them with a BBQ lighter and a can of aerosol hairspray."

"You mentioned fire before, I remember that now. There's also something else. I had a dream about you." The mental image was faint, but it came back to Debbie as she spoke. "It stands out in my mind now that I'm talking to you. You're a man made of gold."

"Sure, thank you. That's very nice of you to say."

"But you were surrounded by a shadowy figure that whispered darkness in your ears. Who is that?"

Debbie saw GT freeze at this last statement. The man stared at her for a moment, his mouth opened, then closed. He tried again, and a single word came out: "Zaleos."

"Zaleos? What- Who is Zaleos?"

"Perhaps I was right about you after all." GT said. "I need some time to think on this. Please be safe, I'm sure we will meet again." Abruptly he turned and walked out of the hospital. Debbie watched him go, then shook the thought of him from her mind. Her girlfriend needed her, she had to return to her side. It took another hour, but May was able to naturally pass the toy, and she was discharged from the hospital. Debbie drove May home, then she texted Gerard to let him know she was OK. Debbie pretended to be a rebel, but deep down she was a responsible, sensible girl.

CHAPTER FIVE

Debbie turned the page of the scrapbook. She chuckled as she saw the next entry. "A bookmark from that library. I still remember the book you checked out. You sent rather mixed signals with that one."

"Libraries are my favourite places." May said. "It was nice to go to one with you."

***

Some images only make sense when they appear in a dream. For Debbie the image of Gerard with a sprinkling of dust on his face made a terrifying amount of sense when she dreamed it. It meant he had been still as a statue for an unusually long period of time. And no normal person stayed that still for that long. The feeling of dread gripped her heart even as Gotye's Easy Way Out jerked her from sleep back to the waking world. She took a deep breath to calm down as she rose from her bed and pulled on some sweatpants. It was time for her morning run.

Her jog was uneventful this morning, but the combination of steady exercise with the brisk morning air served to invigorate the young woman. After a solid hour of cardio, she went back to the hostel for a quick shower and a change of clothes. She grabbed a power bar from her bags and bit into it. She wouldn't join Simon for breakfast this morning. The young man hadn't done anything wrong, but Debbie just wasn't in the mood to listen to another long rambling lecture on film history. This morning she headed straight to the garage and found Trixie eager to see her.

"Debbie, thank God! Give me a hand with this lug nut!" The older woman was struggling with a seized nut on her front wheel. At Trixie's request, Debbie held the wrench steady while the older woman stomped her foot on the wrench's far end. Trixie's ample weight combined with the torque of the wrench to loosen the nut, and Debbie was able to unscrew it.

"Thanks for standing up for me yesterday." Debbie said. "Andre and Hai-man were being real jerks."

"Oh that? Don't let that get to you. They're just young and hot headed. All boys go through a phase like that. My own son was like that at one point himself. It twisted me in knots for a while, but I just rolled with the punches. He grew out of it. Those boys will too."

"You're really proud of your son, aren't you?"

"You bet! I've made some real screw ups in my life. But I like to think mothering is one thing I got right."

"I've been thinking about that myself. Being a mother. It's different in a lesbian relationship. I mean for a straight couple, a man and a woman have a child. And that child is biologically linked to both of them. But for a lesbian couple, only one of the women will get pregnant, and we would need an outside man to cause that impregnation. So, one of the partners isn't biologically linked, and there's a person outside of the relationship involved. I do want to raise a child someday, but I wonder about these details."

"That's nothing too out of the ordinary." Trixie said. "My parents divorced when I was young, and my stepfather wasn't biologically linked to me, but he raised me right. And I divorced my husband, but we also raised our child right. The biology ain't so important. Just get a man to donate. Hell, there's no shortage of men willing to let someone else raise their kids."

"I know I have options. Like I could get an anonymous donor at a clinic or something. But I wonder how that would impact my child as they got older. They might want to try to seek out their biological father. Ideally, I'd like a man who would be supportive of me and my partner. A man who would respect our situation, but also still want to be a part of his child's life. I'm pretty close to my father, and I'd like my child to have a positive male role model in their life too."

"Well, that would be a very particular type of man." Trixie said. "You might be expecting a bit too much from a fella. Making a lifetime commitment to have a child is no small simple thing. You'd better be prepared to have arguments over how to best raise the kid."

"Well, it'd still be mainly our child, even if the father is involved. I'd want him to be close and supportive, but still respect that my partner and I would have the final say."

"Well, what's in it for him? He's not getting laid and he can't control how his kid is raised. What does he get?"

"Well, we'd handle the financial stuff, for a start. And we'd take care of the nasty stuff like changing diapers."

Trixie suppressed a snort. "Any man who cares about those kinds of details is probably going to be a crappy dad."

"OK, but there's other things we could offer. I mean he'd still be the father of our children, so in a way he'd be family. If that man got sick, we could take care of him. Or if he really needed help, like he was feeling really low, we could support him."

"So, this fella will have two young women caring for him when he's most vulnerable." Trixie cocked her head, cynically. "Do you realize there's a chance he'll fall in love with you? You thought about how awkward that'd be, since you wouldn't love him back? Or there's also a chance he'll start thinking he has some kind of blank cheque with you. So, he just gets it in his head that he can mooch off of you for a lifetime. I'm guessing either of those would be less than ideal for you."

"Well, we'd look for that before the pregnancy. That's the point of choosing the right man. For example, we could avoid the issue of the man falling in love with us if we found a gay man who was willing to do this. I don't know anyone off the top of my head, but that's one possibility. For the other issues, well, we'd just judge the man's character."

"Straight or gay, men are still men. You also got to realize people change over the years. Hell, my ex was a sweetheart when I first met him. At one point in my life, I was convinced we'd be happy together forever. But he's my ex now, and he's my ex for a reason."

"Well, sure. But since you're talking about exes and split families, there are tons of men who have children with women. Those men divorce but remain friends with their ex-wives and they all raise their kids together. So, an arrangement like that can be done, it's done all the time."

"Yeah, but those guys don't go into relationships hoping they'll end in divorce. Those men all fall in love too. Getting a divorce and splitting kids with an ex is an unplanned outcome. Those guys are just making the best of a bad situation for the sake of their children. I'm not saying it can't work out for you, girl. I'm just saying I think it'll be harder for you." Trixie stifled a yawn as she spoke. "Sorry, Debbie, didn't sleep great last night. And this is pretty heavy stuff to talk about so early in the morning."

"I know, it's just been on my mind. I haven't really talked to someone about it before. Figured you might have some insight, as a mother yourself."

"Well, what about your own mother? You never asked her?"

"Oh God no!" Debbie flinched at the idea. "My mother- she's- well she's conservative about a lot of things."

"Say no more." Trixie said with a laugh. "There's no shortage of conservative women in Iowa." Debbie finally pulled the rusted lug nut from the wheel and stood up from the bike. She heard the door to the garage open and saw Andre in the doorway. That in itself was not unusual. What was unusual was the hulking beast immediately behind him.

The beast generally looked like a hairless wolf. However, it had six legs instead of four. The front and rear legs looked relatively normal, though they ended in what appeared to be monkey's paws instead of wolf paws. The limbs in the middle looking more like the segmented appendages of a crab than anything belonging to a wolf. Debbie took this all in at a glance, the sight sending a shiver down her spine. Uncanny valley, that was the term for something that looked almost normal, but just different enough to be creepy. She shouted a warning to Andre, causing him to turn. The young man threw up his arms just as the beast leaped for his throat.

The monster's wolflike jaws closed on Andre's upraised arms. Fortunately, the young man wore a thick leather jacket as part of his motorcycle gear. This thick leather caught the teeth of the beast as it hit Andre with a heavy tackle that slammed him to the ground. Debbie still held the wheel wrench in her hands. Normally she would have reservations about hurting an animal. But this particular animal looked alien and was violently attacking a person she knew. Debbie rushed forward and swung the wrench in a low arc, like a golfer. Debbie was in good shape, and the force of her blow was magnified by the momentum of her run from one side of the garage to the other. The steel wrench struck the side of the fiend's skull, and the impact drove the beast off of its prey.

The monster rolled off of Andre as the young man scrambled away from the sudden attack. Debbie had hit it hard, but the beast recovered quickly, and now it began bounding towards the young woman. Debbie had a split second to react. She dove out of the path of the speeding creature, swinging the wrench in a frantic motion as she did so. She struck the monster with a glancing blow, but it was enough to knock it off balance and send it careening into the garage tool cabinet. The beast hit the cabinet with enough force to dent its thin metal shelves and spill tools on the ground. Once more the monster reoriented itself, showing little injury. It leapt for Debbie again, but this time there was less distance between them. No chance to dodge out of the way from this attack. The best the young woman could do was raise the wheel wrench, catching the tool between the jaws of the beast. Even as she did so she felt the momentum of the monster slam into her, driving her to the concrete floor.

The impact of the fall knocked the wind from Debbie's lungs. It was all she could do to keep her grip on the ends of the wrench as the snarling monster drooled and snapped mere inches above her. Debbie gasped for breath as she felt the weight of the monster bear down on her. She felt crushed by the beast, as it struggled above her. Drool sprayed from the monster's open mouth, and its breath stank of rotten meat. Abruptly the horrible moment was over, as the monster suddenly went limp and slid off of Debbie. The young woman looked up and saw Trixie's hand on the handle of a screwdriver. The older woman had stabbed the screwdriver into the beast and sunk the metal shank into its neck. Debbie wriggled out from under the dead weight of the creature and got to her feet.

There was a moment of terrible silence as Debbie, Andre and Trixie stood staring at one another. None of them spoke. What had just happened was too unreal. A monster that wasn't of this Earth had just

entered the garage and tried to kill them. Debbie felt her heart beat violently in her chest. She looked from Trixie to Andre and back again. The silence was interrupted by Simon, who suddenly opened the door to the garage. All three of them looked at Simon, and he shrank back under their unified gaze. "What, is something wrong? Why are there tools scattered all over the place?"

"This thing came in, like this monster thing." Debbie said. "It had giant teeth. It was snarling and vicious. It just bounded in and tried to bite us."

"What, like a big dog?"

"Well..." Even as she spoke, Debbie found herself struggling to remember exactly what she had seen. "See for yourself it's right over-." Debbie turned back to the corpse of the monster, but all she saw was the dented tool cabinet and scattered tools. "It was there."

"What was there?" Simon asked. "What exactly happened?"

Debbie heard Andre speak as she continued to look around the garage. She saw no sign of the monster's corpse. "Well, it was like a big dog thing. But I mean... No, I guess... I guess it was a big dog."

"So, a big dog came in here and made a mess?" Simon asked.

"Yeah." Andre sounded confused, but as he spoke his tone became more confident. "Yes, that's what happened. I guess it's gone now. Must've run out when we weren't looking."

"Well, we should probably clean the tools up before Gerard gets here. It'll only take like a minute." Simon bent down to clean up the mess.

Gerard, the name brought back Debbie's dream for an instant. She felt she was missing something important. A memory just beyond her reach. But she couldn't place it. As she struggled to remember, her cell phone buzzed. May had sent her a text, she wanted to meet at the library a few blocks from her house. Debbie helped clean up the mess of tools, then gave her bike a quick once over. It took a few minutes, and by that time everyone had come in. She looked around and saw Andre, Trixie, Simon, and Hai-man. The same people she had traveled with for quite some time. But today she wouldn't be riding with them. She had a date with May.

Debbie drove up to the parking lot of the library and found May waiting for her outside the front doors. At the Romanian girl's invitation, the couple went into the library and began browsing the books. "I like romance books, even if they are a bit silly." May said. "The men in them act too soft, but it still describes a nice adventure. The books help me imagine an escape from life. Normal life is so restrictive. I am still living with my parents. I have to live by their rules."

"You still haven't come out to them, have you?" Debbie asked. She felt more comfortable discussing this with her girlfriend today. "They still think I'm some friend of yours, and we go together to flirt with boys or something, don't they?"

"It is not easy being honest about such things. Not easy for me, at least." May said.

"It wasn't easy for me either." Debbie said. She saw May turn back to her in surprise.

"No? But it is different in places like North America. I thought it is easy there."

"Not for me it wasn't."

"What happened for you?" May asked. Debbie thought back to that night. The night she had finally decided to come out to her parents. It had only been a few weeks ago, but already she felt detached from the memory.

It was a long plane ride from Canada to Australia. It felt like a rite of passage, the official end to Debbie's life as a student. She had been in school almost her entire life, but with the completion of her psychology degree she finally felt like an official adult. As an adult, she would finally tell her parents the truth. It had been an easy decision to make during the flight. She rehearsed what she would say multiple times as she flew 30,000 feet above the Pacific Ocean. When she landed and saw her father waiting for her at baggage claim, her confidence wavered.

"Howdy stranger!" Father greeted her with a hug. The warmth and familiarity of the experience brought a wave of childhood nostalgia back. Suddenly Debbie didn't feel like an adult. She felt just like her Daddy's little girl again.

"I missed you, Dad."

"How does it feel to be a proper academic?" Her father knew her suitcase by sight and plucked it off the baggage conveyor as he spoke. "Would you prefer to be addressed as Lady Ryans?"

"Oh, shut up." Debbie gave her father's shoulder a playful slap. "It really doesn't feel like anything. I mean, I'm proud to be a uni grad, sure. But I just feel like the same person."

"You mentioned over the phone you didn't want to go to the graduation ceremony?"

"No, they're going to mail me my degree. I gave them our address here. I figured the actual ceremony would be a waste of time. I'd already spent four years on campus, I'm kinda done there." Debbie spoke with a dismissive tone, but the last four years had been pretty good for her. She had been able to live independently and comfortably. The campus had had a vibrant and supportive LGBTQ+ community. She had been able to be honest about herself to those around her for the first time in her life. She hadn't gone out of her way to advertise her sexuality, but people seemed to know and accept it anyways. She had even had some solid relationships. They hadn't lasted, but they'd ended amicably. It had been a nice stage of her life, but now that it was over, Debbie didn't want to linger. As much as she'd enjoyed her time there, she felt the adult thing to do was to move forward.

"Well, if that's how you feel, that's fine. Really though, I don't think the ceremony would have been so bad. I could've taken a few pictures of you for our family album." Debbie heard a touch of regret in her father's voice. She looked up to find him shaking the thought from his mind and smiling back at her. "What am I saying? It's the degree that counts. We can take fun pictures anytime."

"I'm sorry Dad, I didn't think of that."

"No no, it doesn't matter." They walked out of the airport together and Debbie saw her father breathe a sigh of relief. "Whew, am I glad to be out of there. You know the place is haunted right?"

"What do you mean?"

"When the airport was first constructed, they commissioned a local company to install the support beams and sidings. The man in charge was a known penny pincher, and he demanded his crew rush the job so he wouldn't have to pay as much. One of the workers was still installing piping in the interior walls when the crew sealed him inside. He screamed for help, but nobody heard him. He banged on the walls with his wrench, but the other guys just thought it was the sound of someone working. Everyone went home, leaving him to slowly suffocate over the weekend. They say his ghost still haunts the interior of the airport. You can still hear his wrench banging on the solid walls, begging for release."

"What, really? Who was this guy?"

"The papers called him Dan 'Tradesman' Taylor, ghost of the wrench."

"Oh my God!" Debbie laughed at the absurdity of the name and swatted her father on the shoulder. "I actually believed you!"

"Hey what do you expect from your old man?" Father too was laughing. "Half the job of being a dad is telling lame jokes and corny ghost stories." They walked together to father's truck. It was a Ford F550 upfitted with a mechanic body. Debbie got into the passenger seat, on the left side of the truck. She was still getting used to the fact that Australians drove on the left side of the road. Her father had clearly adjusted fine as he got behind the wheel and started the engine. "So, what are your plans now?"

"Well, I've really wanted to travel for a long time. And now that I'm done uni, I mean, I'm finally free. There's this motorcycle tour I saw online that looks kinda cool."

"Yeah, that sounds fun." Her father said as they pulled out of the airport parking lot. "But I meant more long term. What kind of job opportunities do you see in psychology?"

"Well, a psychology degree isn't that marketable, to be honest. I took it because some of the courses were interesting and easy to pass."

"Right." It was a simple word, but the way her father said it broke Debbie's heart. "Well then, what are your career plans?"

"I haven't really made any plans. Figured it was best to concentrate on one thing at a time. So, when I was at uni, I just focused on getting the degree."

"Getting a degree that isn't marketable." Her father said the words gently, but Debbie heard the disappointment in his voice. She felt guilty, like she had let him down. She hadn't even given him her big news and already he was upset. How would he react to the declaration that his daughter was a lesbian? Would he be even more disappointed? Debbie felt herself shift uncomfortably in her seat.

"Where's Mom?"

"She had a headache. She's waiting for us at home." Debbie knew her parents well enough to know when her father was lying. Her mother didn't have a headache. Her parents must have had some kind of fight that caused mom to stay home. Debbie wondered if the fight had involved her, somehow. Her train of thought was interrupted by her father changing the subject. "But that's neither here or there. You should know overall we've been doing great. Business has been booming for me over here. Diesel mechanic services are in high demand, I've been pulling in some seriously juicy paydays."

"That's really great, Dad." Debbie began to relax again. That was the father she was used to. The hardworking man with a fun sense of humour. The man who somehow always seemed to be completely confident and in control. How did he do it, Debbie suddenly wondered. A man like her father always knew how to handle things. He seemed to just instinctively find high paying work to provide for everything. Now that Debbie was an adult, she was learning how difficult it really was to earn the money to pay for a home and a family. Her father had always made it look easy.

"You know the crazy part of this business is the customers you often get. I mean the trade itself, the mechanics of working with diesel engines, that's no big deal. Once you get good at something? It's a breeze! But the customers that you see sometimes, it's just crazy. I had this one guy who insists the Earth is flat. He would demand I keep an open mind as he lectured me on how the world is a disc. How a global conspiracy keeps us from reaching the edge, that's lined with ice. I'd ask him simple questions, like what causes solar and lunar eclipses under his model of the solar system. He'd tell me he didn't know. But at the same time, he'd tell me absolutely without a doubt the world is flat. He just wouldn't see the contradiction in his world view. And you know the funniest part?"

"What's the funniest part?"

"This guy works at the airport! One location where you'd think they'd know the shape of the Earth."

"That's crazy." Debbie forced herself to laugh even as she felt her anxiety build. They were pulling into the driveway of their home now. She recognized it from pictures her father had sent. Debbie braced herself. Mother was inside, and once they were all together Debbie would have to tell them the truth. It was like ripping off a band-aid, the young woman told herself. She just had to get it over and done with. The longer she waited, the harder it would be. She would just have to do it once, and it would be done forever. Her father parked the truck, engaged the brakes, and led her into the house.

Debbie was silent as her mother greeted her at the front door. The older woman gave Debbie a perfunctory greeting and then immediately turned back to the kitchen. Mother was already preparing dinner, and that process occupied her attention. But there was an abruptness to the older woman, one she exhibited when she was in a bad mood. Debbie looked to her father for reassurance, and he saw the uncertainty in her eyes. That was his cue to change the subject. "You know another funny thing that happened? I had this customer who was a complete control freak. I was working on his vehicle and he wouldn't stop hounding me, telling me how to do my job. Now you know me, I'm a pro. I take it all in stride. But this fella, he wouldn't stop buzzing around me like a hummingbird. He was just full of energy. He practically vibrated with excitement as he told me to check a filter and adjust a plug. Well, I'm under the engine and he's shaking his head like a madman, when I hear a sudden tink of glass breaking. Turns out the fella got so excited he shook the glasses right off his head. The lenses broke on the cement of the shop floor. The guy is legally blind without his glasses and can't see ten feet in front of his face. I had to stop everything and call his son to come pick him up and drive him home. Maybe it's just an Australian thing, but I've never seen a guy get so worked up over a simple engine repair."

"Yeah, that's nuts." Debbie said, forcing herself to smile. Her father was a comforting presence. His voice was familiar and his habit of telling silly stories was something reassuring that Debbie had known since childhood. But she felt uneasy, and not just because of her mother. This new home in Australia felt strange to her. She recognized some of the furniture from their Canadian home. That helped in a way. But at the same time the contrast between what she found familiar and what was new to her was disconcerting. This house was larger and more expansive than what she had grown up with in Canada. In a way it was a reminder that her childhood was over. That she had to get used to changes as she got older. Her parents were familiar, but now that she was an adult their relationship was different. The same way this new house had some familiar details but was itself different. Her father guided her to a room in the house, and that compounded the problem. This new room had her childhood bed, her childhood dresser, her childhood desk, and on the walls her parents had placed the same pictures.

As her father left to help mother with dinner, Debbie took another look at the pictures on the wall of her new bedroom. Her father had bought them for her when she was 10 years old. She had read "Treasure Island" around that time, and that book had fostered an unhealthy fixation with pirates. Watching a DVD of the film "Pirates of the Caribbean" with Johnny Depp had cemented that fascination. And so, with a love of sailing the seven seas, Debbie had walked with her father through a store filled with posters and pictures. Her attention had been drawn to two specific pictures of ships from the 1700s. She didn't know the names of the vessels, or their functions. All she had seen was ships standing proud on the ocean, providing the promise of adventure. That had been enough. At her request a purchase was made, the pictures were framed, and they hung proudly on the wall of her bedroom.

Debbie looked at them now, with the eyes of an adult. As a child they had represented adventure and daring. But as an adult she wondered about practical details. What types of ships were these? Who had commanded them? What specific year had these ships been commissioned and what was their specific purpose as they sailed across the ocean? All of these questions flitted through Debbie's mind, and even as she looked at the pictures, she considered her own thought process. Why were these details important, all of a sudden? They had never mattered to her when she was a child. She had just used her imagination to make up answers to those kinds of questions. Why couldn't she do that now?

Looking away from the walls, Debbie surveyed the rest of her room. She remembered years at her desk, either studying for school or reading for fun. She remembered afternoons on her bed, often on her phone. Perhaps talking to Liz, sharing some funny viral video with her. Then Debbie would go to her dresser, pull on some sweats and jog around the neighborhood. Except the neighborhood she remembered was across the globe. She didn't talk to Liz anymore. She was done studying too. As a child, Debbie had been eager to grow up. Now, in this familiar but different room, she wondered why she'd been in such a hurry.

As a child, and even into university, Debbie had focus and structure. Now she had no idea where her life was going. She had no plans, simply an endless, overwhelming new world that she had to make her way through. It suddenly felt like too much, Debbie had a sudden urge to hide under the covers of her childhood bed. But even as this irrational feeling gripped her, she remembered she did have a plan. She planned to come out to her parents tonight. To finally get it over with and be true to them. Once she was out of the closet with them, she was officially out completely. That was her next step. It was only a plan for tonight, but it was a start. Grasping at this new goal, she was able to focus and calm herself. She would get through tonight, one way or the other. And after dealing with that challenge, she could face the next challenge life had to offer her. Debbie's train of thought was interrupted by the voice of her mother, calling her down for dinner.

Debbie emerged from her new bedroom to find a familiar aroma waiting for her. She smelled pot roast, a dish her mother cooked on special occasions. She knew this meal. It was complimented with

mashed potatoes, green beans, chopped carrots, and slathered on top
with her mother's home-made gravy. This was the meal her family
made for holidays like Christmas and Easter. Her mother might
have been in a bad mood, but she had made the effort to prepare a
nice meal for her daughter. As awkward as this homecoming felt,
Debbie recognized this effort. In her own way, her mother was doing
something nice.

Debbie walked down from her bedroom, and her father guided her to
their new dining room. It too was larger than in their old house. Her
parents had also gotten a new dining table. It was fashioned entirely
from oak, sturdy and solid. Debbie felt her father's warm hand on her
shoulder, guiding her to the table as they sat down to eat. He had been
telling a joke, she remembered that much. At this moment, the details
blurred together. The joke had been related to father's work. They had
begun eating, and Debbie had tasted the roast beef.

Abruptly, Debbie stood from the table. This uncharacteristic move
was enough to silence her father. Her mother, who was used to formal
manners at the table, was equally shocked by this sudden interruption.
Debbie still had partially chewed roast beef in her mouth. She took
a split second to swallow, then began her prepared speech. "I have
something to say. It will be a surprise but I know you love me and want
me to be happy. I'm gay. I've known for years, but I've been afraid to
tell you. I'm not confused about this. I've had a few relationships with
women now. I don't want to lie to you anymore, this is who I truly am.
I'm a lesbian. I date women. Your daughter, Debbie Lauren Ryans, is
a gay woman." The words flew out of her mouth in one long rambling
statement.

It had been a speech Debbie had practiced for some time. Short,
honest and to the point. In her mind she had pictured saying it to her
parents, she had gone over the words time and time again. But she
hadn't planned on how her parents would react. She had hoped for
warmth and understanding. That perhaps they had already known and
had just waited for her to say it out loud. But instead, the speech was

greeted with silence. Debbie saw her father's jaw drop, and there was a look of disappointment on his face. Abruptly he too stood, turned from her and stomped to the other end of the dining room. His arms were crossed over his chest, his head was lowered. Debbie watched him walk aimlessly towards the dining room wall, unsure of what he was trying to accomplish. She felt her heart sink in her chest while her father turned his back on her. She was completely unprepared for her mother's hands around her neck.

Her mother had been silent and still, causing Debbie to focus on her father. But as Debbie turned her head away, the older woman suddenly lunged. "I raised a worthless dyke!" The words dripped from her mother's mouth like acid, burning into Debbie's memory. They hurt, more than the hands that were currently shutting off Debbie's airway. The young woman was too stunned to react as her mother violently shook her back and forth. It was a horrible moment, but it was only a moment. Suddenly her father was there beside her, his strong hands tearing Debbie free.

"What the hell is wrong with you?" Father said. "That's our daughter!"

"I have no daugh-."

"Don't you dare finish that sentence!" Father interrupted. "Debbie is your daughter. Debbie will always be your daughter. We love her and support her no matter what! That's it!"

Abruptly mother left the room. Debbie felt a moment of shock, unable to process what she'd just experienced. Then she felt tears began to trickle down her cheeks. Too much emotion, all at once. She felt her father's reassuring arms around her, and she hugged him close. Father spoke, his voice familiar, his words reassuring. "You OK, sweetie?" Debbie nodded, although she felt too choked up to speak. "Let's go for a drive. That helps me feel better when I have a lot on my mind."

The sun was already setting as Debbie followed her father to his truck. They drove silently for a while, at night Australian roads didn't look too different from Canadian roads. They were still driving on the opposite side of the road, but Debbie could ignore that. Her father joked that they never did get dessert, so they got some ice cream. They ate together as he parked the truck off the side of the highway. "I'm sorry if I got weird on you, sweetie. I live in the 21st century. I know it's OK to be gay. It's just a shock to hear it from a close family member. It feels weird, like everything I knew about you was a lie. Like you're a stranger with my daughter's face. I'm sorry, I know that sounds horrible, but that's honestly how it feels. But then seeing your mother do that-. Well, that was a quick reminder that I'm your father and I have responsibilities. It's different seeing someone else treat you like that. It puts things back into perspective. I'm not saying this exactly right, but I hope you know what I mean."

"Yeah, I get it." The words hurt, but Debbie knew her father well enough to know he meant well. When discussing something serious the man spoke bluntly, his words honest and direct, because he always believed a hard truth was better than a comforting lie.

"Look, in my mind I know you're the same wonderful young woman I've raised all these years. It'll take me time, but I'll get over my shock." Father was silent for a moment, as he looked out at the Australian darkness. "In the meantime, I never did properly reward you for getting your degree. You've mentioned several times you've wanted to travel. Business has been really good lately. How about we look into a trip for you, for your graduation gift?"

"That would be nice." Debbie said. "There was this motorcycle club I mentioned earlier. It's a tour around Europe. I think it could be a positive experience."

"Well, there we go." Father said. "Let's sign you up, and I insist you let me pay for everything. You'll go on a new adventure, have some fun. I'll talk things over with your mother. When you get back, we'll be right back to normal again."

They went home and powered on her father's computer. They logged onto the ECE website and found an open spot for her. They were lucky to get her a flight that would leave the very next day. It looked expensive, but her father insisted that didn't matter. The next day he was driving her back to the airport. Debbie didn't see her mother throughout all of this. They did speak over the phone after her plane landed. Mother's voice sounded strained, as though she was speaking through clenched teeth. But her mother at least admitted that she had overreacted, and she apologized. Debbie had accepted the apology. It was her mother for crying out loud, what else was she going to do?

"And that's why I'm touring Europe now." Debbie said as May looked up at her. "Why I was lucky enough to bump into you."

"Your mother is strict." May said.

"Well, she's old fashioned. She grew up in the southern part of America, even though she moved with my father to Canada and then to Australia."

"My parents are strict too." May said. "I don't want them to choke me."

Debbie didn't know how to respond to that. The memory of her mother's hands on her neck still haunted her. Though it had only been a few seconds, it had been one of the worst experiences of her life. But she liked to think she'd done the right thing. Her father preferred a hard truth to a comforting lie and coming out as a lesbian had been one of those hard truths for him. Debbie hoped that by being honest with her parents, their relationship would be stronger moving forward. She didn't know May's parents though, not really. She had no idea how they would react. So, she would have to trust May's judgement. If May felt it was better to remain in the closet, that was her decision.

"I like this book." May pulled a volume from the shelf and brought it to the checkout desk. Debbie glanced at it and smirked. It was a copy of Carmilla, the 19th century vampire book that predated Dracula. At the checkout desk, the library had complimentary bookmarks, and May took one as she signed the book out. "I will read it when I am at home. I will think of you."

"I'll assume you meant that as a compliment." Debbie said as she raised an eyebrow. Carmilla was a book famous for its strong lesbian undertones, but the titular character was still a monstrous killer. Debbie wasn't sure if being compared to such a figure was entirely fair.

CHAPTER SIX

Debbie turned the page of the scrapbook and the next entry puzzled her. All she saw was a few shards of rock taped to the page.

"This is flint rock, from that stone place we walked." May said. "When you tell me about roofing, that job you had."

"Oh, I remember now." Debbie said. "I had a lot on my mind that day. So, I'm sure you'll understand why I didn't immediately get it."

***

Gotye's Easy Way Out pulled Debbie from a dreamless sleep back to the waking world. She groaned as she stretched in her hostel bed. For a moment she felt tempted to just curl back up in a ball of warmth. Drift back to sleep and hit the snooze button on her phone every five minutes until the sun was high in the sky. But she managed to resist the temptation. She had gotten into a good routine, and it was important that she stick with it. Groaning a second time, Debbie rolled out of bed and pulled on her sweats and fanny pack.

The morning air was cold in her lungs and her feet beat a steady rhythm on the pavement. She had good shoes, that was essential. A friend of hers had once developed shin splints while jogging, and to hear it told they made every step complete agony. That had made Debbie conscious of the importance of quality footwear as her feet steadily pounded the pavement. A familiar voice suddenly interrupted her train of thought. "Debbie, do you have any salt?"

The young woman turned in the direction of the voice and saw GT stooping in an alley. The grubby man appeared fixated on some kind of nest or growth. She walked forward as she dipped her hands into her fanny pack. "Actually, I do in my pack." Her jogging had made her alert, but for some reason part of her mind felt like it was just waking up as she spoke to GT. "I remember now, I bought packets of salt, a lighter, a folding knife, and I still have the silver spike you gave me. I'm not sure exactly when I bought those, but they've been in my pack this whole time. I had bottled water, but I think I drank that at some point."

"Can you pass me the salt? I need to neutralize some Muco Daemon Involuta."

"What's that?" Debbie asked as she handed the packets to the young man.

"It's a fungus that occurs when demons permeate our world. It is malleable and used by demons for several purposes. In this case it is evolving into a nest for more Parvulus Hirudo. They chose a better spot to manifest in this alley. There will be more human traffic for them to infect, and then metabolize into Malae Turbela. I told you about that before, but you might not remember."

"No, it's coming back to me now." Debbie watched as GT sprinkled salt on a growth of pulsating tissue in the alleyway. Upon contact it began to shrivel and die.

"It will vanish soon, as do all demons once they are neutralized."

"That's a demon?"

"Yes, though not a very advanced one. Hell seems to have its own ecosystem; it needs more primitive demons to support the more advanced and deadly soldiers of the damned. I've read some details on how this system operates but my knowledge is incomplete, and I don't understand fully how these creatures interact and develop. Part of it could be demon magic, though I've heard it said magic is just science we don't yet understand. The fact that these fiends dissolve back to hell soon after they die makes them harder to study." Even as GT pointed, Debbie saw the shriveled tissue fade from her sight.

"I think that happened before. There was this dog thing in the garage." As Debbie looked into GT's eyes, the memory came back into focus. "No, not really a dog. It was larger, had weird hands and like a crab leg."

"That is a Belial Lupal. A demon legion that serves as a basic minion under almost any ranking demon of the peerage. It's named after Belial, one of the most powerful kings of Hell and first demon created after Lucifer."

"How about that guy you mentioned earlier, Zaleos. Is he a King too?"

"No, he's a Duke."

"What's his deal." Again, the image came back to Debbie's mind. GT personified as a golden figure, wreathed in a smokey shadow that whispered in his ear. "He speaks to you somehow, right?"

"Zaleos whispers to me fairly often, yes." GT said. "If that fiend is to be believed, my grandfather summoned him and made a deal with him. He is somehow linked to me through a familial bond I don't understand. But he is a peer and rival to Astaroth. It serves his interests to see his rival fail. So, the duke constantly whispers to me to keep me focused on my task, alleviating Astaroth's mind control effects. It's a symbiotic relationship in this case, because for obvious reasons I want Astaroth to fail to take over the world as well."

As Debbie listened to GT list these facts, a different thought came to her mind. "GT, don't take this the wrong way, but are you autistic?"

"I don't know." GT spoke without inflection. He didn't look offended, he answered frankly and honestly. "It's possible, even likely. You're not the first woman to say that about me. I've never been tested for autism. There's no point, really. As long as I can effectively thwart Hell it's not relevant."

"I'm not judging you or anything. But the emotionless way you speak. The way you list things." Debbie hesitated a moment. "Your smell kinda implies you have an unusual sense of hygiene." She winced as she said this. GT didn't react, but she felt rude saying that. She anxiously tried to change the subject. "I just, I recently graduated university with a psychology degree. I remember studying a bit about autism. It's nothing bad, it just means you have a different kind of mind. I mean, hey, I'm a lesbian. I'm different too."

"You studied psychology?"

"Yeah, you don't need to tell me. It rivals philosophy as one of the most useless degrees I could get."

"I never went to university." GT said. "I was homeschooled, and my education consisted almost entirely of demonology."

"You're not missing much." Debbie laughed. "Going to university is just what a middle-class girl is supposed to do after high school, and psychology was interesting. At least at first. It got tedious towards the end, but I stick with it to get the letters by my name. Call it sunk cost fallacy. I know I'm an idiot for not studying something more marketable, you don't have to tell me. I'm probably going to end up working in the trades like my dad. So apart from being able to sign BA after my name, my psychology degree is a joke."

"Psychology is the scientific study of the mind." GT said. "You realize Astaroth is a demon that utilizes mind control, don't you? Psychology might not be marketable, but I doubt it's completely useless."

"Well to be honest, I didn't really take it all that seriously. University was just an excuse for me to party and socialize. It was my first time away from home, and the first environment where I wasn't afraid to come out of the closet and be honest about my sexuality. I spent more time finding myself than really going to classes. I mean I crammed for the tests, and I passed them. But I didn't really retain all that much."

"What do you remember about your studies?"

"Off the top of my head? Let me think. I guess some things stand out. I remember the structure of the neuron. It has axons, dendrites, synapses forming a gap between. I remember reading a bit about the history of psychology. There was Carl Jung, and a guy named Skinner who made the Skinner Box. Pavlov and his dog. I remember Sigmund Freud was a stupid overrated hack who cared more about his career than about the welfare of his patients. That's why he came up with ridiculous crap like the female Electra complex, or the idea that men want to bang their own mothers. Even the dumbest person could tell you those concepts are idiotic. They contradict the Westermarck effect."

"Please focus, Debbie. I don't think the history of psychology is relevant to countering Astaroth."

"Right, sorry. There are four basic types of memory: Working memory, sensory memory, short term memory, long term memory. There's this idea of chunking memory. That's where you memorize really large groups of information by sorting it into smaller recognizable groups."

"Now we're getting somewhere. How can you use that to beat mind control. Specifically mind control that affects the memory?"

"You mean like amnesia?" Debbie thought for a moment. "I remember reading that amnesia tends to go away on its own. Some forms of dementia can be alleviated by medication. Also, there have been doctors that used hypnosis to extract repressed memories. But the efficacy of that technique is controversial."

"I've read about demon hypnosis. It is used to make a victim docile and more prone to mind control. The idea that hypnosis can be used to combat a demon's power is interesting. I will have to think on that."

"Sometimes certain rituals can be useful in imprinting memories as well." Debbie said. "Repetitive behaviour can help develop muscle memory."

"Rituals? Like prayer?"

"Yeah, I guess."

"I didn't think of that, but now it seems so obvious." GT said. "There must be prayers and rituals used against a demon like Astaroth, specifically in response to his mind control. Eternal demons don't innovate, they stagnate. Astaroth has used the same trick for his entire existence, making him predictable. His powers must have been studied and tested by the angels and saints that have opposed him. I can't believe I missed something like that."

"OK, glad I could help you out there." Debbie said. "Anything else you need, while I'm here?"

"I want to subdue one of Astaroth's lieutenants: Glasya-Labolas. The author and captain of manslaughter and bloodshed. He is mindless and violent. I'm wary of facing him alone. I'm pretty sure I know where to find him, and I could use an ally like you to watch my back. But I'm concerned you won't remember anything after we finish talking. How could I contact you?"

"Well, I tend to jog the same route every morning. If you find me and explain things, I'm sure I'd be lucid enough to help you. Just prepare me beforehand."

"I am good with preparation." GT hesitated, and to Debbie's surprise she saw some real vulnerability in his eyes. "The idea that you could help me, when I'm going to face something terrible. That really means a lot to me. Thank you."

"You're welcome." The words came reflexively. It was all Debbie could think of to say. She was beginning to feel tired again, detached and numb.

Abruptly Debbie felt a warm hand grip hers. She saw she was hiking along a forest trail. She looked to her left and saw May walking beside her. It came back to her now; they were going down another trail in the Carpathian Mountains. They had walked in the mountains before, but it was a large area to explore. They could walk through the mountains for weeks and not cover the same trails twice. A moment of confusion came over Debbie, she didn't know where she was. But the morning details also came back to her as she focused. She had woken up, gone for her run, and eaten a power bar for breakfast. She had dressed, had gone to the garage. The same general routine she'd had for a few days now. She had briefly said hello to the other bikers, looked over her bike, and picked up May a block from her home. They had driven together up into the mountains to be alone. She remembered the route now, and the stop they'd chosen. Then they had just walked together for a while. It had all been a blur, but time often flew when things were going well.

"You look really pretty today." Debbie told May, making the young Romanian girl smile. "Of course, you look pretty every day." This comment made the girl's smile even wider.

"Debbie, you are good girlfriend. But sometimes I don't think I am good girl for you."

Debbie paused and turned to May. She placed her hands on the Romanian girl's cheeks gently. Their eyes met, and Debbie savoured the moment briefly. Then she kissed her girlfriend full on the mouth. There was passion in that kiss, but then tenderness, followed by gentle warmth and affection. Debbie slowly pulled back from May and smiled. "May, would I kiss you like that if I didn't think you were the most wonderful girl in the world?"

May blushed and turned away. The reaction was adorable, and Debbie couldn't help but fall in love with the sweet innocent girl. She still held May in her arms, and she gave her a quick hug before releasing her. May was quiet and shy. But that was OK. Debbie liked to talk, and a good talker is complimented by a good listener. As the two women walked along the trail, Debbie saw something to talk about. There was an unusual rocky outcropping that sparked a memory for her. "You see that solid formation of rock? It makes me think of a summer job I did a few years back."

"You want to tell me about it?" May asked. "I like learning more about you."

"As a university student, I studied in the spring, winter and fall. For the summer I was supposed to get a job. I didn't really need it; my father made good money and paid my way. But he wanted me to work to at least get the experience on my resume. So, I took a job roofing in the summer."

The memories came back to Debbie as she spoke. She had taken to roofing exceptionally well. She wasn't scared of heights, and her first day on a roof she had been as solid as a billy goat. She remembered the man she had been partnered with; a grungy worker named George Deen. George had been abrasive, and condescending. He had bad breath and politically incorrect views on migrant workers in Canada's job market. But he had also taught her the basics of the trade. He had taught her how to hold and carry massive 30–40-foot ladders. The trick was to hold them upright, perpendicular to the ground. Hold them at an angle and the weight and torque of the ladder would be too much to bear. He had also told her about the use of lanyards and harnesses. He had suited her up and led her to the edge of a roof. Then, while they had both been secure, George had beckoned her to look down at the drop below. Debbie had done as instructed, but exhibited no fear, as she had faith in the harness securing her. To her satisfaction, she saw George show visible frustration at her bravery. The jerk had wanted to make her flinch.

To George's credit, Debbie could clearly remember one laudable thing he had done. There was a moment where they had worked together on a barn roof, replacing shingles. Debbie had lost her footing and began sliding down the slope of the roof. George, further down the slope from her, had seen her slide and anticipated her momentum. She saw the older man lean back and slam himself into her. The collision arrested the momentum of her slide, halting her movement. She was able to recover and regain her footing. If George hadn't intervened, Debbie might have slid off the edge of the roof and tumbled to the ground below. As awkward as the moment was, Debbie had to admit technically George had saved her life. Or at least saved her from injury. He was still a condescending jerk, but he had helped her out in that moment. She had to give him that much.

It had been a long summer, but Debbie had learned more working with the roofers than she had learned from multiple years at university. She still remembered the importance of fall protection. She remembered how to remove rotten shingles from a roof. Basic applications of roofing sealants, coatings, and mastic asphalt. She remembered how to maintain her balance on uneven surfaces. She was a decent student in the classroom, but she always found she learned more working with her hands. One thing that had stuck with her throughout that job, she wasn't afraid of heights. But there was another thing she remembered; she was the only girl who had applied for that job. It was an industry almost entirely dominated by men. Even though George had been an asshole, he had still taught her the basics of the trade. Other men seemed cautious of even speaking to her.

So many times, Debbie remembered hearing her fellow workers talking and laughing good naturedly as a group. But as soon as they saw her coming over, they would immediately become silent. They would nod to her respectfully, ask her how she was doing, and wish her a good day. But the men would not feel comfortable opening up and speaking to one another naturally until they thought she was out of earshot. Then they would tell dirty jokes, tell lies about the sex they were having, and advise one another about how to succeed with both business and women. This appeared to be how men spoke when women weren't around. Though Debbie had good hearing, she only caught glimpses of this culture. But she saw that there was a man's world in the industrial trades. It was possible she might try to one day to build a career in a trade like that. She wondered how difficult it would be, to be fully accepted into such a culture.

"I have to wonder about how fair it is." Debbie said to May as they approached the rocky outcropping. "Women have their spaces where they talk about things, including the shortcomings of men. So, isn't it fair that men have similar areas where they feel safe being themselves and talking about women? But at the same time, it's a work environment that should be open to everyone. Women rarely work in the trades, but I'm different than most women." Debbie still remembered how it felt to see those men abruptly shift from natural conversation to awkward silence. It didn't matter how hard she worked, or how friendly she was. Her coworkers always treated her like an outsider. She remembered one occasion when a young man had approached her directly and asked her permission to tell a dirty joke. Naturally she had permitted it. But it made her think. While the older men were often more set in their ways, the younger men were usually more respectful. But younger men timidly tiptoeing around her seemed demeaning in a whole other way. A way she couldn't really articulate, because at least these young men were trying hard to be nice. It was frustrating to think about it, because deep down she knew there was no easy solution. You can't force people to think a certain way, or to accept things they aren't prepared for. You can't force someone to open their mind, any more than you can force a flower to bloom by prying open its petals. As these thoughts crossed her mind, Debbie realized May was still looking at her. "I don't know. I guess the short answer is we should all just try to be respectful to everyone. Being able to compromise and come to an agreement is a valuable skill. I think that skill applies in every workplace."

"I don't understand everything you say." May said. "But I agree compromise is good." Debbie watched as the Romanian woman approached the stony outcropping. She reached forward with her slim hand and tore a section of flint from the formation. "This is good for me. Important, I think." Debbie didn't understand how a few shards of rock could be of any significance. But if it was important to May, that mattered to Debbie. She wanted to be a supportive girlfriend.

CHAPTER SEVEN

D ebbie tasted blood in her mouth and felt her top incisors with her tongue. They were loose, shifting in her mouth and about to fall out. She must have hit her head, though she didn't remember when. All she knew was that she had to get to a dentist or she'd lose her teeth forever. It was nerve wracking looking for help. All around her were strangers who didn't speak English. Somewhere, Gotye's Easy Way Out was playing. Must be from a nearby shop. If there was a shop, there might be someone working there who spoke her language. Debbie looked around, but she couldn't tell where the music was coming from. Everything was shadows lit by a glowing orange hue. She pushed her teeth in harder, they felt looser. The music kept playing, but she couldn't find where it was coming from.

Debbie sat up in her bed and felt for her phone. The alarm hadn't woken her up like normal, her mind had incorporated it into her dream. Debbie checked her teeth, they felt fine, although she still remembered the loose sensation she had dreamed of. She remembered reading that dreams of losing teeth were an indication of stress. That wasn't right, Debbie thought as she pulled on her sweats. She was on vacation. The whole point of a vacation was to alleviate her stress. She tied her shoes, and out the door she went.

And she bumped right into GT, who was waiting for her outside of her hostel. "Good morning, Debbie. Are you ready?"

Debbie stared at the grubby man for a moment in shock. It was weird that the guy was waiting right outside the place she slept. Was he stalking her now? Abruptly the memory returned to her. "Oh, that's right. You asked me for help."

"My Dacia is parked around the corner. This early there won't be much traffic. We should reach our destination in about 20 minutes." The idea of getting into the car of a strange man made Debbie flinch. But as she looked into GT's eyes, she relaxed. He was a good person, she was sure of it. And she had talked to him several times now, they were becoming friends. She followed him to his car, and they drove together out into the mountains. "I told you before Glasya-Labolas is the embodiment of manslaughter. You might not have realized it, but he's killed several people, including someone you know. He's a lower demon of the peerage, taking the form of a dog with the wings of a griffin. But he'll be covered in a slimy organic tissue called Pituita Cortex that will obscure his appearance."

"Wait, he embodies killing but he's one of the lower demons? Wouldn't Hell consider killing someone to be the ultimate sin?"

"Manslaughter is a crime of passion, done in the heat of the moment." GT said. "Greater evil is accomplished through careful planning and cold calculations. I know it's cliche to bring up the Holocaust, but it's a good example as that atrocity was organized through careful planning. Astaroth is a planner, whereas the mindless urges of Glasya-Labolas forsake these plans for short term gratification. Astaroth has been trying to keep him on a short leash-." Here GT broke off, chuckling. "Heh, leash. I did say he takes the shape of a winged dog. Anyways, while Astaroth has been trying to slowly tighten his grip on this region through subtle mind control and corruption of the environment, Glasya-Labolas has been violently killing innocent people, and encouraging other demon legions to follow suit. He's a detriment to

Astaroth's subtle machinations, but he's still causing death and needs to be stopped."

"OK, so you got a gun?"

"Conventional weapons won't hurt it. It can be wounded, but not killed, with silver. I have a collection of sterling silver blades and spikes in a pack in the backseat. We need to get in close and stab the fiend. That would be the best way to immobilize him. Then we'd need to peel the Pituita Cortex from him and expose him to the air. Demons of the peerage that haven't been directly summoned melt when exposed to the air."

"So, this guy wasn't summoned?"

"No, Astaroth was the demon directly summoned. He'll need to be banished with a ritual. But his ranking lieutenants go down more easily. At least in theory." GT took a deep breath. "But there always seems to be some kind of cost to banishing a ranking demon. I've done it three times now, and I've lost something every time. It's why I'm nervous about doing this. I am grateful to have you by my side." With that final statement, GT pulled the car over. He put his finger to his lips and pulled his pack from the backseat of the Dacia. He passed Debbie two silver objects. One was an antique sterling silver butter knife with the blade sharpened to a razor's edge. The other was another silver stake sharpened to a point. GT took two similar weapons for himself. Together, they quietly exited the car.

GT led the way, walking quietly along a wooded mountain path. Debbie followed, gripping her weapons tightly. She felt she could trust GT, but the man was apprehensive. Although he looked disheveled, and smelled a little strange, there was still something about him that radiated strength. If he was nervous, then she was nervous. As Debbie considered this, GT abruptly stopped walking. Debbie saw the man square his shoulders and grip his silver weapons tightly. It was still early in the morning, and quiet on that mountain. GT shattered this silence with an abrupt roar. "I've found you, Glasya-Labolas! Kill me or I will kill you!" Then GT charged forward.

Ahead of GT, Debbie saw something swoop down from the trees. GT had said the demon was a winged dog covered in slime. Debbie had a split second to take it in as teeth erupted from the slimy tissue of the monster's head and gnashed at GT's throat. At the last minute, the young man juked to the left, swinging his arm down in a stabbing motion as he did so. GT's strike had interrupted the monster's flight, and it tumbled down to the dirt. The demon was back on its feet immediately, but Debbie saw GT had stabbed silver into one of its wings. The demon spoke then, with a low gravelly voice. "You dare challenge me? I'll tear out your throat and your arrogance will be forever silenced."

GT's provocation had been a clever tactic, Debbie thought. The demon was an embodiment of murder through passionate rage. An enemy that is too overwhelmed with fury to think clearly is an enemy that is easier to beat. With this in mind, Debbie quietly walked up behind the demon as it spoke and stabbed with her own silver spike. She buried it in the left cheek of the demon's butt. A crippling blow, as well as a demeaning one. The demon turned faster than the young woman had anticipated, and bit out at her even as she snatched her left hand back. The demon drew blood, but only barely. Debbie pulled away her left hand and slashed out with her right. She scored a glancing blow on what appeared to be the demon's lower neck. She was surprised to hear Glasya-Labolas emit an agonizing shriek. A wide gash of the Pituita Cortex was peeled away, exposing the skin beneath to the open air.

The demon reared back on its hind legs, and GT caught it in a low tackle. The man wrestled with the beast for a moment. With his left hand he secured the demon's head, limiting the monster's ability to lunge and bite. With his right hand, GT began to peel. The demon began to smoke, and Debbie could smell an aroma that made her think of a candle being extinguished. The demon appeared to deflate in

GT's arms, like a balloon slowly leaking air. After a moment, all that remained was the slimy Pituita Cortex tissue. GT stood and extracted the silver weapons. He turned to Debbie. "We got him. Are you OK?"

"I'm fine, yeah. That was intense."

"He's strong, but impulsive. A fairly easy combination to beat, if you know what you're doing." GT led the way back to his vehicle. "You're sure you're alright?"

"I'm a big girl, you don't need to worry."

"Well as I said, every time I've dispatched a ranking demon, something bad has happened. So, I'm just a little concerned, that's all."

They drove back to Debbie's hostel. She hadn't actually done her morning run, but that was OK. Taking on a monstrous demon was enough of a workout for one day. Debbie went to the garage and saw the rest of the crew already prepping their bikes. Closest to her were Andre and Hai-man while further off she saw Simon talking to Trixie. The young woman cringed as she saw Hai-man rise from his bike to greet her. "Look who finally got out of bed. Your girlfriend must've worn you out last night."

The mocking tone combined with the mention of her girlfriend to make Debbie's temper rise. She felt her skin flush and she clenched her fists. "Why do you keep messing with me? You wouldn't speak this way if Gerard was here." It suddenly occurred to her that it had been a while since she'd seen Gerard. She was confident these young men would mind their manners in the presence of a reasonable male authority figure.

"Oh what, you're gonna go tattle?" Andre asked. "What are you, ten?"

"You're just always so disrespectful. It's obvious you look down on me because I'm a lesbian."

"Hey, I love lesbians." Hai-Man said. "Your porn is fantastic." At this statement, Debbie clenched her left hand so hard it throbbed. She remembered she had a folding knife in her fanny pack. In that moment it was all she could do to keep from flipping out that blade and burying it in the man's throat.

"It hurts me that you would take something important to my identity and reduce it to a cheap fetish." Debbie spat out the words, her voice overwhelmed with both anger and pain. To her astonishment she saw Hai-Man's smile slip, and for an instant his eyes softened.

"Hey, he was just kidding." Andre cut in.

"Oh, that's super convenient, isn't it?" Debbie said. Her hand still throbbed, her face was still flushed, but she made an effort to keep the emotion out of her voice. "The words 'just kidding' are the perfect get out of trouble free card. Act like a raging jackass, then just say those two magic words and be absolved of all accountability."

"This coming from a woman." Andre suppressed a laugh. "You live your whole life free of any real accountability."

"What's that supposed to mean?" Debbie asked. "That doesn't even make any sense."

"Never mind."

"No, I need you to actually explain what in the screaming hell you meant by that. Obviously, there are consequences to a woman's actions. Everyone has accountability. What were you even trying to articulate with that statement?"

"Let me put it this way: You cry rape, people come running. I cry rape, people laugh. You claim you were sexually harassed, people investigate. I claim I'm sexually harassed, people tell me to grow up. You say the wrong thing, people dismiss it. I say the wrong thing, I get hit. That clear enough for you?"

Finally, Debbie was able to understand what the man meant. She remembered a discussion on gender in one of her courses where a similar point was raised about victimization. While Andre was oversimplifying complicated gender roles and ignoring the challenges women faced, she was now at least following his train of thought. Debbie tried to be a kind and understanding person, even when the person she was talking to didn't really deserve it. She took a deep breath, she forced herself to unclench her fists. She would try to meet Andre halfway. "OK, that's a fair point. Male victims are not taken seriously, while female victims are. It comes at least partly from a societal view that women are weak and need defending, and that men are worthless and disposable. It's an attitude that is offensive and demeaning to both genders. It's unjust. More should be done to teach people that pain and suffering are always serious no matter who the victim is."

Now it was Andre's turn to express surprise at Debbie's words. He had clearly expected Debbie to shout him down, not to make an attempt to see things from his point of view. Before he could respond, movement out of the corner of his eyes caught his attention. "Oh God, Mighty Mouse is here to save the day." Andre smirked as Simon stormed over to join the conversation. "Look at you, buddy, stomping over here like you're John Wayne."

"More like John Wayne Gacy. You guys need to be nicer to Debbie."

"Oh, so you're threatening to kill us? Smooth, real smooth. That kind of talk really impresses the ladies. How do you see this going down in your head, kid? There's two of us, we're bigger than you, we each got like 60 lbs. of muscle on you, and you can't fight for shit. Are you thinking you're going to just knock us out with one punch and carry Debbie away into the sunset?"

"That's not going to get you laid, bro." Hai-Man said. As the taller man saw Simon about to speak, he clarified. "Yes, we all know Debbie is a lesbian. I mean in general that kind of thing won't get you laid. Life isn't a movie. You don't just beat up the bad guys, save the girl, and live happily ever after."

"You know what, we'll do you a favour." Andre threw up his hands in mock surrender. "You're totally too intense for us, you've scared us off. Enjoy your victory, see how far it gets you."

Debbie and Simon quietly watched the two men go back to their bikes. Debbie breathed out a sigh. "Listen Simon, thanks for trying to stick up for me. It's sweet that you care. But in a weird way those guys are right, you don't need to get into fist fights for me or anyone else."

"I was just trying to-."

"I know, I know, and I appreciate it." Debbie gave Simon a friendly punch in the shoulder. "But I can take care of myself. If I'm ever seriously in trouble, I'll call out, OK?"

"Sure, OK."

Debbie watched Simon go back to his bike. Her hand still pulsed, causing her to examine it more closely. She had been cut recently, though now that she thought about it, she couldn't remember how. It wasn't deep, but it could still use a bandage. Debbie went to a first aid kit hanging on the garage wall and took out some gauze. Even as she dressed the injury, it pulsed once more. The mild pain brought a momentary surge of anger. It didn't make sense, but for a split second she really wanted to strike out at someone. Words suddenly burned in her mind: Lacerate, mutilate, silence the laughter with death. She shook the hideous thoughts from her mind. She didn't know why she was in such a horrible mood. She had a picnic date with May today and her girlfriend had promised her a surprise gift. Debbie was certain May's warm energy would make her feel better.

CHAPTER EIGHT

With her bandaged left hand Debbie turned the page of the scrapbook, and saw it opened to a blank page. "The rest of it is blank."

"Yes, it is symbol of our relationship. We have so many more memories ahead to share. We will fill the pages together."

"This is really a wonderful gift. Thank you." The two girls sat together in silence for a moment. "You mentioned you had something you wanted to talk to me about."

May turned away from Debbie then, shifting her gaze to the mountain view. Debbie read the Romanian girl's body language; she could already tell this was important. May was a shy and submissive girl, and her English wasn't perfect. It took May a few attempts to even begin speaking, and often she would have to pause to find the right words, but gradually she was able to tell her story.

Before Debbie, May had had one real relationship. A man named Florin Muller. She had met him roughly a year ago, and felt immediately drawn to him. He had a fast car, played bass guitar, and had a recreational opiate habit. In her naivete, May had considered him an outlaw rebel with a heart of gold. He took her for a few dates, which mostly consisted of driving her around. Their fourth time together, he took her to a bar. She didn't remember everything they talked about, but eventually the conversation drifted to his use of opiates. He liked to mix them with his drinks. May had lived a sheltered life, and the idea of experimenting with drugs had a certain romanticism to it. She knew they were bad for her, and they ruined lives, but she couldn't help but be curious anyways. It was something forbidden to her, which made it all the more fascinating. She shared this with Florin, and the young man took this as an invitation to prepare her a drink. When he gave it to her, she thought it was just a normal drink. May had been overwhelmed by a powerful sensation of euphoria. But that feeling of pleasure was mixed with confusion, fear and helplessness, and it ended in a blackout. It was like her mind had gone to sleep for the night, but her body had kept going. It was mostly a blur, but she remembered little glimpses of feeling through the haze.

She woke up in a motel bed feeling sicker than she'd ever felt in her life. She saw Florin passed out in the other bed across the room. She remembered stumbling to the bathroom, vomiting into the toilet. Through the pain and sickness, May realized Florin had hurt her and betrayed her trust. In that moment, she felt numb. May came back from the bathroom. She remembered gathering her things that had been strewn about the floor. Then she had quietly left the motel. She remembered walking in the cold and the dark for a little while, before the realization of what had happened to her finally began to sink in. That someone she had really cared about had betrayed her trust. It was a feeling that would haunt her for a very long time. She walked all the way back to her parents' home, getting there just before sunrise. She never told them what happened. She never told anyone. Debbie was the first person she had trusted with this.

Debbie listened silently, nodding and making sympathetic noises. She reached forward with her right hand, placing it reassuringly on May's shoulder. Her left hand she clutched in silent rage. It pulsed in time to her heartbeat, and again the words echoed in Debbie's mind: Lacerate, mutilate, make him pay. Outwardly, Debbie controlled herself. She spoke to her girlfriend in measured tones. "Where is Florin now?"

"I've watched him on internet, I know he works at a bar in the next town."

"I want to confront him." Debbie said. She wanted to do more than that. She wanted to cut his throat, watch the blood drain from his body, and leave him for the animals to drag away into the woods. His corpse would never be found. "He needs to know what he did to you is wrong."

"I don't- I don't know." May said. "It was hard just to tell you this. I don't think I can face him."

"Just take me to him. I'll take over. He needs to be taught a lesson." Debbie still saw doubt on May's face. She chose her next words carefully. "Think about it. If he's done that to you, he's done it to other girls too. It's important we put a stop to that."

"Yes, I- OK, I think that is true."

The two girls packed up the scrapbook and picnic supplies. They got on Debbie's bike and rode down the mountain. Debbie drove fast, but the trip still took over two hours. She didn't care, her rage steadily burned, her left hand pulsed as it gripped the handlebars. The sun was just setting as they reached the bar. It looked like a slow night, because the bar appeared to be almost empty. She saw only one man arranging bar stools inside, who must be Florin. Less witnesses, Debbie told herself. Her thoughts were interrupted by May, who spoke with a sudden confidence. "I will go inside."

"You will?" Debbie thought about it for a moment. "Yes, that makes sense. You go in and lure him out. I will take care of things."

"Well, maybe." May said. "Now that I see him again, and I know you are outside waiting to protect me, I feel more brave. For so long I have been so scared. But Debbie, you are helping me to have courage. I want to confront this, I want to face him." Debbie watched as May walked forward. She was surprised at the Romanian girl's sudden initiative. But Debbie knew this was important to May. May felt she needed to be the one to face that horrible man first. Debbie would wait outside, ready to cut his throat as soon as he let his guard down. It was a reasonable plan, a plan Debbie could work with. As she watched May enter the bar, Debbie slipped the folding knife from her fanny pack into her left hand. She felt her hand pulse as it gripped the blade, in time with her beating heart.

May entered the bar, scared but determined. It took Florin a moment to recognize her, but what happened next was something the young woman was not prepared for. Florin dropped what he was doing and called out her name with surprise and delight. Then he rushed towards her with his arms outstretched. The sight of the man who had hurt her suddenly rushing towards her was more than May could bear. Abruptly she screamed "Nu!" The Romanian word for no. A simple, abrupt command, but one sufficient to halt Florin's eager advance. The young man hesitated for a moment, but then began to speak in an excited tone.

He hadn't seen her for over a year. A lot had happened since then, but he had missed her so much. He had thought about her almost every day. He remembered having a wonderful night with her, then waking up to find her gone. His life had gotten darker since then, but he had always hoped he would have a chance to see her again. He had felt a real connection with her. She had been a brief moment of happiness in an otherwise dark time in his life. He didn't know why she had left, but now she had suddenly come back. He would love a second chance to rekindle what they had shared.

May took all of this in with bewildered silence. It sounded alien to her, completely different than the man she remembered. Just as Florin finished his impassioned speech, the young woman finally found

her voice. She told him he had hurt her, hurt her so badly she'd had nightmares of him. At these words, the smile vanished from Florin's face. He stood across from May, uncertain what to say. Finally, he asked her what she meant.

Suddenly May felt angry, and this anger gave her fresh courage. She remembered Debbie was waiting outside, supporting her. She didn't need to be afraid of this man anymore. She spoke in a louder voice. Florin had drugged her. He was the reason she had woken up sick and stumbled home in the cold darkness. What kind of monster was he to treat another person so horribly?

May saw Florin's face change from uncertainty to distress. That wasn't how he remembered it. He had given her a drink with opiates because he thought that's what she had wanted. He had been drunk and high as well, and he thought they were sharing a beautiful experience together. They had stumbled to a motel, but they slept in separate beds, nothing happened. Florin hesitated as he spoke, thinking for a moment. Florin admitted that time had shown him how horrible his opiate habit really was. And it was wrong to have introduced May to that darkness in the first place.

There was an awkward silence between the two for a moment. Then May spoke again. She was surprised to see Florin listening to her, she didn't remember him being this sensitive. But it felt good to tell him how she really felt and have him respectfully acknowledge what she was saying. She told him that her experience with him had hurt her in a really horrible way. That it had been hard for her to trust anyone in the last year because of him. That she was only just starting to get back to normal. Florin stared at the floor in silence, and it took May a moment to realize he was struggling not to cry. Instead, he silently nodded, once more indicating he understood what she was saying. May spoke again, suddenly remembering what Debbie had told her earlier. She wanted Florin to promise he would never give drugs to anyone ever again.

Florin took a deep, quivering breath, and when he spoke his voice was strained. He told May a lot had happened to him in the last year. His opiate addiction had caught up to him, and he had gone to a rehabilitation center to deal with his habit. He was clean now. He didn't do drugs anymore. He even abstained from beer, although he still held down a job working at his friend's bar. Lifting his head, he looked May in the eyes. He promised her he wouldn't do it again. Then he said he was sorry.

May stared at Florin silently for a moment. Up until this moment she couldn't imagine how it would feel to have this man apologize to her with genuine sincerity in his voice. She didn't know how much she needed to hear that. It felt like a crippling emotional burden had just been lifted from her. And looking at him now, she began to remember why she'd fallen in love with this man in the first place. The danger that had made him so attractive at first was gone. But there was a kindness and sensitivity to him that remained. Slowly, she began to nod in acceptance. Once more she spoke. She told Florin that she had hated him for over a year. But after tonight, she didn't hate him anymore. Then May turned and exited the bar.

Debbie saw none of this, all she saw was May walking out of the bar alone. "What happened?" Debbie asked. "Where is he?"

"It's OK." May said. "Florin he- well he apologize to me."

"That's it?!" Debbie almost screamed. Her hand pulsed a staccato beat, still clutching the blade. She saw May's eyes glance down at the weapon.

"Put that knife away, are you crazy? Were you going to kill him?"

"He's a monster! He deserves nothing less."

"I don't want to kill him. I hope you respect me enough to make that decision. Now put that knife away. I tell you already." May said. "I did not think you were this kind of person."

Debbie folded the knife and slipped it back into her fanny pack. "I just wanted to do what was right."

"You don't know everything." May's expression suddenly softened. She took Debbie in a warm hug, and kissed her. "But you do something wonderful tonight. You bring me here, support me so I can confront him. Talking to him, it finally give me peace. I only have that peace because of you. Thank you, Debbie."

Debbie still felt conflicted. Letting a monster like Florin go just because he had apologized, that didn't seem right. Her left hand still pulsed. She wanted to slice Florin's throat and feel his hot blood soak her as she laughed. That was justice, surely it was. But May was holding her close, the Romanian girl's warm touch took away some of Debbie's rage. The two women embraced silently, then went back to Debbie's bike.

CHAPTER NINE

In a world of distorted shadows, cast by glowing deep orange light, Debbie found herself surrounded by horrible people. They were all laughing at her, belittling her. Mocking her for things she couldn't help. Some of them had gotten away with horrible crimes. Some of them were sadists, who wanted to hurt and belittle her just because they could. All of them had some sin of their own that made them rotten, and all of them were laughing at her. It was unjust, but she could see that nobody cared. Nobody but her. Debbie was alone, but she wasn't helpless. She could silence their laughter. She could destroy their evil. Looking at her hands she saw she was gripping a blade. Small and sharp, it wasn't much, but it would do.

Debbie stabbed, she slashed, she sliced. The cruel smiles, the mocking laughter, it was all abruptly cut short as she thrust her blade into their wretched faces. She was rewarded with a torrent of hot blood that steamed wet against her face and soaked her up to her elbows. It was deliciously satisfying, an experience rather like popping giant pimples, only magnified several times. Faces flashed in front of her now, faces of men who had angered her at one point or another. Those faces needed to be cut apart. She lashed out at Gerard, Andre, Hai-man, even Simon. Yes, that little twit tried to be nice, but he was endlessly annoying. Who would be next? What about her mother, who had called her a dyke? Her friend Liz who had used her and cast her aside. Everyone was horrible, everyone deserved to die. She saw another man in front of her, a face she recognized. It was her uncle Adam, his kind face wearing an expression of concern. He hovered in front of her in the darkness, his familiar voice echoing in her mind. "This isn't like you. You're a good person."

"But they're all awful, everyone. They've hurt me, they need to pay."

"I've known you all your life. This isn't who you are. You're better than this." Debbie felt the rage seep out of her as her uncle's words flowed through her. "You're not a killer. Lashing out like this, that's the easy way out."

Abruptly, Debbie woke to Gotye's Easy Way Out, playing on her phone's alarm. She had just had the weirdest dream, although now she was only remembering parts of it. One detail stood out distinctly: The feeling of hot wet blood soaking her arms. That part specifically had seemed so real. Debbie brought her hands up, but was relieved to see they were clean. There was a small cut on her left palm, but it had already scabbed over and was healing nicely. The dream had been intense, she could only assume it had been brought about by her concern for May.

As she sat up in bed, Debbie thought over her actions last night. She had actually sent May into a bar to lure a man out to the woods. She had actually planned to cut that man's throat. It seemed incredible now, but last night she had been prepared to kill someone. It had seemed like the right thing to do at the time, it had felt like justice. She had never even considered an action like that before. Certainly, Florin was a horrible man, but killing him? That wasn't who she was. The idea of leaving his body dead in the woods, she was so glad that hadn't actually happened. She knew that memory would have haunted her the rest of her life. Even if she got satisfaction in the moment, she knew herself well enough to know that guilt would slowly overwhelm her as time went on.

Debbie took a deep breath and pulled on her sweats. She needed to focus on the reality of her situation. She had almost done something crazy, but almost only counted with grenades and horseshoes. She hadn't actually done it. That meant she could just forget about it and go back to living her life a free woman. She couldn't regret something that hadn't actually happened. With this in mind, the young woman went out for her morning jog.

Normally Debbie jogged for about an hour. But she had missed her workout yesterday, and she had a lot on her mind this morning. So today she would extend her workout to over an hour and a half. It took her a minute to recall why she had skipped yesterday. She had done a favour for that guy GT. The memory was a blur, but she remembered helping him catch a dog up in the mountains. Debbie pushed the thought away as she increased the pace of her run. It was cold this morning, unseasonably so. She'd warm up if she pushed herself a little harder. This extra effort combined with the extra duration of the run to push the young woman to her limit. She was soaked in sweat by the time she returned to her hostel. A strenuous effort, but a rewarding one.

Debbie showered off the sweat, then pulled on an old pair of jeans and a flannel shirt with short sleeves. Remembering the cold, she pulled an old leather jacket from her luggage and tugged it on. The jacket would keep her warm, and it was durable motorcycle safety gear. She fished a power bar out of her luggage and chewed on that as she left the hostel. She didn't feel like eating a heavy breakfast today.

Entering the garage, she saw Hai-man rise to meet her. "You seen Andre?" Debbie shook her head, still munching on her power bar. "He's not here. We've hung out every day of this trip. It's weird, he wouldn't just take off without telling me."

Debbie shrugged. "Well, he's your friend, not mine. I don't know what to tell you."

"How about Gerard? Where's he been this whole time?"

"I don't know, I've been with May. I always took off early to hang out with her, and texted him later in the night. Figured he was touring with the rest of you. You haven't seen him?"

"No, the last few days we've all been doing our own thing and texting at the end of the night, same as you. Me and Andre mostly just rode around town and chatted up girls. We found a few that spoke English." Hai-man shook his head, realizing he had gotten off topic. "Anyways, we have a scheduled itinerary for this tour. Weren't we supposed to leave Romania today?"

"Oh, that's right. I forgot all about that. What am I going to do about May? Maybe I can talk to Gerard about staying longer." Debbie pulled out her cell phone and dialed Gerard's number. She waited anxiously as it rang, and to her relief he didn't pick up. "Looks like he's busy, so there's probably some kind of delay. I think we can assume we're here a little longer. I should still call May though." Debbie pressed another button on her phone, dialing May's number. May didn't pick up either, but Debbie didn't feel the same relief. Should she drive to May's house? Her thoughts were interrupted by Simon walking into the garage.

"Hey Simon, you seen Andre?" Hai-man asked. Simon shrugged in reply. "Well how about Gerard? When's the last time you've seen him?"

"Haven't really been keeping track." Simon said.

"I'd like to know what our travel plans are." Debbie said.

"Gerard usually comes in a bit later." Simon said. "I want to adjust the pressure of my tires and look over a few things. Let's wait a bit. I mean Trixie hasn't come in either." Walking passed them, Simon went to look over his bike. Debbie watched him go and turned to her own vehicle. Simon was probably right. Gerard wasn't the kind of person to just disappear. Andre, maybe, but Gerard was a reliable guy. Debbie rolled up her sleeves and looked over her bike.

As they went through their routine, Trixie came into the garage. She hadn't seen Gerard or Andre either. Once more Debbie tried calling Gerard, once more he didn't pick up. She glanced at the time, it was close to 10:30. "He's got a room at the hostel, right? We can just go knock on his door." Simon, having finished with his bike, walked over to join her.

"Yeah, I know where his room is." Simon said.

"OK, why don't you guys do that." Hai-man said. "We'll wait here for a bit. I'm sure it's no big deal. I'd just like to know what our new schedule is. If we're just going to be riding around Romania for the rest of our lives, I can live with that. The girls here are cute."

"I can appreciate that, Hai-man." Debbie laughed.

"Right, I wanted to say..." Hai-man suddenly faltered, showing a touch of frustration. "I know I gave myself the name Hai-man. It seemed kinda funny at the time. But the joke has gotten a little old. Do you think you guys could just call me Emmanuel or Manny from now on?"

Debbie nodded understandingly, then she followed Simon to the hostel. Her legs still ached a bit from her run, but she was in a good mood. She just wished May would pick up the phone. She dialed again, but once more there was no answer. Simon led her to the third floor of the hostel, to a room at the end of the hall. He rapped his knuckles on the door. There was no response. He knocked harder, then tried the knob. To their surprise, the door budged open. It was locked, but the latch didn't quite catch. "Should we go in?" Simon asked.

Debbie stared at the door for a moment, then pulled it shut. The latch still didn't catch, but at least the door was closed. "No, that's a violation of his privacy. We're not the cops, we don't have a warrant or anything. All I wanted to know was what his plan was. But that doesn't make it OK to just bust into his room."

"Yeah, cool. We tried. So what now?"

"Well, usually I hang out with May." Debbie said. "But she's not picking up today. I could drive by her place, but now that I think about it, she had a sort of crazy night last night. I think maybe I should give her some space today."

"So, you're free?"

"I suppose I am, Simon."

"Have a drink with me."

"What, now?" Debbie looked back at her phone again. "It isn't even noon."

"We're just out of college and vacationing in Europe." Simon said. "We're pretty much obligated to get smashed at least once. And I think you'd be a fun drinking buddy."

"I'm not getting smashed." Debbie suppressed a laugh. "I will join you for a modest glass of wine or two. I'm not going to get fall down drunk and start crying on your shoulder."

"Fine I'll drink enough for both of us." Simon said. He flinched back as Debbie punched him playfully in the arm.

"Oh no, you're not getting weepy fall down drunk on me either! I'm a good friend, but I'm not carrying you home." Together they left the hostel and found a bar. Debbie kept part of her promise, she did drink wine. But she failed to limit herself to two glasses. She was just finishing her third glass when a memory from this morning returned to her. "You know I had a dream this morning. I don't remember much, but I remember Liz was in it."

"Yeah, you mentioned her before. You watched Easy Rider with her."

"She was my best friend at one point. When we were kids, we hung out all the time. Then in high school we kinda found our own groups, but still hung out once in a while. Mainly we messaged each other online. When I went to university, we only talked online. I really wanted to make an effort to stay friends with her. She used to be so much fun and I wanted to get that friendship back. I kept planning to see her during summer vacation, but she always had an excuse not to see me."

"What kind of excuse?"

"All through University she'd tell me about her problems. Actually, now that I think about it, she was telling me this stuff in the last year of high school too. She claimed to have anxiety and depression. She'd tell me she was bipolar. Then she started claiming to have BPD, then something called Mast Cell Activation Syndrome, or MCAS. She'd tell me problem after problem. I remember feeling so bad for her. I'd listen to her talk for hours on end, and I'd do my best to support her. I'd suggest exercise routines to help her get healthy. I'd offer to take her out to help get her mind off of things. She'd always refuse of course. She just wanted to talk about her problems, endlessly. In hindsight, it was probably some bizarre form of Munchausen's syndrome. Do you know what that is?"

Simon took a moment to think. "Well, it sounds familiar."

"It's basically where you pretend to be sick or hurt so you can get attention. Thinking now, I honestly believe that's what she had. At the time all I knew was that it was hideous to deal with. What I remember most from her is suicide threats." Debbie grimaced at the memory, and filled her glass. "She would jump online, usually like around midnight, and just declare that she was ready to kill herself. Always the same song and dance with her: she wanted to end it all, nobody cared, she just couldn't see a reason to go on. She'd pull this at least once a year, often around Christmas. Looking back, it was basically a holiday tradition for her. But as the years went on, she'd do it other times as well. Every time she did it, I'd take it seriously. I'd talk to her long into the night, often until like 3 or 4 in the morning. It screwed up my own plans, like it made me late for class the next day sometimes, but I thought I was being a good friend. I just imagined her actually killing herself, and being haunted by the idea that I could have stopped it. And on some level, it felt good to feel needed." Debbie scowled, and took a long pull from her glass. "Looking back on it, I was probably an idiot for doing that. It's pretty obvious she just did it for attention, which is disgusting. Threatening suicide is a horrible emotional burden to place on a friend, and I don't think she even cared about our friendship at all. All she seemed to care about was getting dick."

Simon was in the middle of a drink, and that last statement made him choke. Debbie slapped her hand on his back as he coughed for a moment. "What?"

"Liz wouldn't shut up about the men she was crushing on. Dating seemed to be the only thing that gave her life meaning. It never went well for her. She'd be with a guy for a bit, then he'd leave her for another girl. Then I'd have to listen to Liz complain about what a skank that other girl was, and how she could offer so much more in a relationship. Which is a juvenile attitude when you get right down to it. I mean think about it, doesn't matter if you're straight or gay. If your partner is the kind of person to leave their last squeeze for you just because you have more to offer, what's to stop them from leaving you the second they find someone else that can offer them a better deal than you can? If that's all there is to a relationship, then you have a partner with no loyalty or integrity."

"Makes sense, makes sense."

"I kept hoping Liz would figure this out on her own, but she never did. She just kept drooling over man after man, moaning to me about it the whole damn time. This lasted until my final year of university. I was starting to get sick of hearing it, so I tried dropping hints. She ignored them, or maybe my intentions weren't clear on messenger. A lot gets lost communicating through online text messages. You don't see a person's body language, or hear their tone of voice. Regardless, no matter what I tried, that last year was her worst ever. On the one hand she'd claim I was her only real friend. She was going through so much difficulty and I was the only person who still talked to her. But that apparently just meant way more bizarre suicide threats. I remember three times in one month she messaged me late at night. She needed me, she couldn't go on, everything seemed hopeless, blah blah blah! Three bloody times in the span of a month! And I took it seriously every - single - time!" Debbie took another drink, as the memory returned to her. "And then she told me about this latest guy, Todd. Apparently, she'd slept with him once, and never seen him again. He talked to her online, but not in person. He was with another girl, but Liz said what she always says: She has more to offer that man. Todd claimed his current girlfriend was emotionally abusive, or some other nonsense. When I heard this, I did what I thought a good friend should do. I told her to forget about Todd. He was clearly just leading her on. He'd had her once, so she was a notch on his bedpost. Now he was stringing her along just so he would have a second option. I thought Liz was stupid not to see that. So, I told her, politely, that she needed to accept Todd wasn't for her."

"Seems fair." Simon said.

"Well not to Liz, it didn't. We'd been friends for ten years. According to her, I had emotionally carried her through some of the darkest moments of her life. But the minute I tell her something she doesn't want to hear, she loses it. She started swearing at me and typing in all caps. Saying I betrayed her trust by being so dismissive of her feelings. Saying she had enough problems, and I was a horrible friend for not supporting her." Once more Debbie grimaced at the memory. "This is the kind of behaviour you expect from a 12-year-old, by the way. Screaming at someone for not blindly endorsing your crush? It's ridiculous, Liz is a grown woman. Then she accuses me of wanting Todd for myself. That's when I felt cold."

"Why?"

"Because that hammered home how little Liz had bothered to understand me. I hadn't made a big deal about being a lesbian, but most people who knew me were kinda able to guess anyways. Not my parents, but that was a different thing. My friends? Most of them knew without being told. But Liz didn't pay attention, because deep down she obviously didn't care about me. She saw me as someone who existed for her benefit. In her mind I needed to be there for her, but she didn't need to be there for me. Just as I realized this, another thought came to me." Debbie paused to take another gulp from her wine glass. "If Liz ended our friendship, I'd never have to hear her threaten to kill herself again. And since it was her choice, I wouldn't have to feel guilty about it either. So, I stuck to my guns. I repeated what I said. I typed it out respectfully, and kindly, but it was still a statement she didn't like: Todd was wrong for her. She told me we would never be friends again, and removed me from her friends list online. It was a relief, to be honest. I waited for a few months for her to change her mind. After a decade of friendship, I felt she was owed that much. Then I blocked her on all media accounts. That was the end of that part of my life."

"I'll be honest, I can't tell the difference between a gay girl and a straight girl myself."

"What do you mean?"

"Well, from my perspective, lesbian girls are just the same as straight girls except they're not interested in having sex with me." Simon took another sip of his wine. "But straight girls don't want to have sex with me either. So, what's the difference?"

That caught Debbie off guard, and in spite of herself she burst out laughing. She wrapped her arm around Simon's shoulder, giving him a friendly hug. "I need to change that. It's not right that a nice boy like you is single. Stick with me after this tour, I want to find you a cute girl who likes you."

"Oh, don't make promises you can't keep." Simon's attention was suddenly distracted by a new person joining their table. "You need something, mister?"

"I was wondering if I could join you for a few minutes." GT's familiar voice made Debbie look up.

"Oh yeah, that's cool." Debbie said. "Simon, I don't know if you've met this guy. This is GT, we've hung out a few times. He's alright."

"I wanted to buy you another bottle." GT said. "On the condition you join me in a short prayer. I know it's a little awkward, but you're my friend and it would mean a lot to me."

It meant a lot to him, Debbie thought. She wasn't a fan of organized religion, and she could tell Simon wasn't either. But if GT needed another small favour, she could respect that. "Alright GT, we'll give you a couple of minutes. I promise I won't laugh."

GT uncorked the wine bottle and topped up Debbie's glass. Lowering his head, he began to pray. "O Saint Bartholomew, you were described by the Christ as a man without guile. Let us too be without guile or deception. In your name shall we see evil clearly. In Saint Michael's name shall we smite evil." GT reached towards Debbie and gently placed a finger on her forehead. He rubbed something gritty on her in a criss cross pattern. Debbie was surprised by the sudden touch, but the wine had relaxed her and to some extent she trusted GT. "Let me now anoint your forehead with salt, in the name of the triune God. Blessed be you, Deborah, and sacred be the wine you now drink, long a symbol of man's covenant with Christ through his blood. Amen."

"Amen." Debbie said, taking another sip from her glass.

"Thank you, Deborah." GT wiped excess salt from his hands. "I can't tell you how- that is to say-."

"Sure, it means a lot to you. I got it."

"What's up with this Saint Bartholomew?" Simon asked. "Any relation to Bart Simpson?"

"Oh, he's the Saint who directly opposes Astaroth, being the only one to conclusively resist his mind control." GT listed the details in a monotone voice. "As a Saint, his miracles have historically involved changes in weight. That might make sense as Astaroth is an air demon. He is also associated with medicine and salt. He is often depicted with a flaying knife that has a silver blade and a gold handle. He is the patron saint of leatherworkers, like those who crafted your jacket, Deborah."

"The Saint of Leather?" Simon asked. "Why that of all things."

"For his martyrdom Saint Bartholomew was ritually flayed before being beheaded. He holds his loose skin in his hands and that is often associated with leather-."

"Ew! What the Hell, GT?" Debbie interrupted.

"Yeah, come on." Simon said. "I'm sorry I asked."

"I apologize." GT rose from the table. "Sometimes I say too much. I didn't mean to upset you. I'll leave you to your drinks." Abruptly, he turned and walked out of the bar.

"That was weird." Simon said. "I mean he seems like a nice guy, looking at him. But seriously, wow."

"Yeah, it did kinda kill the mood. I'm gonna finish this glass and then I think that's enough for one day." Debbie drank the rest of the wine in a steady gulp and rose from the table. She took a moment to steady herself, and began to laugh. "Not a minute too soon. I think I had more than I'd planned. Hey Simon, looks like you'll have to carry me out after all."

"I got you." Simon said. Of course, Debbie was exaggerating, she was a little off balance, but still mostly in control. Nevertheless, Simon supported her with his shoulder and the two walked together out of the bar and into the street. Debbie was giggling the whole way, and she playfully rustled Simon's hair. He was a good friend, when all was said and done. Out in the street, Debbie's giggling died. She stared into the afternoon sky.

"Simon, look up."

Simon followed Debbie's gaze. "OK, what?"

"What do you mean, what? Look!"

"Look at what? What's wrong, Debbie? You sound upset."

"Simon, do you not see that the sky is glowing bright orange?!"

CHAPTER TEN

The entire sky was a flickering orange, as though it was one solid wall of flame. There was no heat and Debbie couldn't smell any smoke. But the longer she looked up, the more terrified she felt. The Carpathian Mountains still loomed over the town, and she saw another distinct object overhead. It was roughly diamond shaped, though it had an organic structure to it, like a giant hive. It hung in the distance over the mountains. Debbie looked back to Simon and saw the drunken confusion on his face.

How could he not see this, Debbie asked herself. Looking around she saw other pedestrians, Romanian townsfolk walking along the sidewalks. All of them looked calm, none of them noticed the burning sky above. Then an obvious solution struck her. She had been drinking, and someone must have slipped some drug into her glass. It had happened to May, and now it was happening to her. Debbie hurried away from the bar, ignoring Simon as he called after her. She was still staggering a bit, but the sudden adrenaline had sobered her to some degree. She was still enough in control to get back to her room, and that had a lock on it. She wobbled as she ran, and got some funny looks, but she returned to the hostel without significant delay. She slammed the door shut, locked it, and turned around quickly.

Debbie half expected to find someone waiting for her, but to her relief she was safe. Debbie looked to the heaviest object in the room, her bed. With a grunt, she slid it across the room and braced it against the door. Then she sat on the bed and took a deep breath. She still felt drunk, but she wasn't about to pass out. She thought of the film 'The Hangover,' where a drug dealer had mixed up hallucinogens with roofies. Had something similar happened to her? Had a predator wanted to roofie her, but slipped some kind of hallucinogen into her drink instead? Or had it been intended as a practical joke, and Debbie had just taken off before the prankster could reveal themselves? If it was a joke, Debbie wasn't laughing.

Debbie looked around her room one more time, including under her bed, to make absolutely sure nobody else was there. The only way into the hostel room was the door she had locked and braced. She was safe enough. She could just sleep off the wine and drugs and wake up normal tomorrow. This plan made sense to her as she lay back on the bed, but she couldn't help but still feel nervous. She closed her eyes, focused on deep breathing, and slowly began to relax. It took time, but sleep did come.

Debbie woke up with an aching head. Groaning she crawled out of bed, wishing she'd had the foresight to drink some water the night before. She checked her cell and saw she had slept through her alarm. It was almost 8am. She was a mess. She hadn't even undressed or brushed her teeth. Debbie promised herself she would never drink again, but that was an idle promise for anyone in their 20s. Debbie grabbed her towel, a fresh pair of jeans and a t-shirt. No jogging this morning, she'd skip right to her morning shower. Debbie struggled to open the door, before realizing she needed to move the bed away. That was odd, but she had been drunk. Debbie was just happy she hadn't lost her phone or keys. The young woman staggered to the communal washroom. She peeled off her old clothes, showered, brushed her teeth, and dressed. This routine made her feel a little more normal as she exited the Hostel. Then she looked up and saw the sky was still burning.

"You see it, don't you?" Debbie turned to see GT standing by the entrance. "It worked, it actually worked."

"What? Where did you come from?" Debbie had several questions, but that was the first one to come out of her mouth.

"Sorry, I wanted to talk to you. I knocked on your door, but I guess you were sleeping too heavily to hear me. I didn't know what else to do so I waited around for you to wake up. I was hoping to talk to you earlier, after I saw you looking at the sky, but you rushed off."

"You did this to me? What, did you drug me?"

"No, this is what things actually look like right now." GT said. "Everyone in the area has been mind-controlled to be complacent. The ritual has opened your eyes, removing the demon influence from you. You were blind but now you see, John 9:25."

This was too much for Debbie. Abruptly she went back into the hostel. It was too early for this. She was hungover, her head pounded. GT was someone she had trusted, and now he'd betrayed her in a really messed up way. He must have been the one to spike her drink. She did not want to be around the man right now. For a moment she considered her options. She could go to the garage, but she'd have to leave the building and GT might follow her. She could lock herself back in her room, but GT might still wait around outside. Besides, she deserved better than to cower behind a locked door for hours on end. She could call the police, but she remembered being told 911 didn't work in Romania. It was a different number here, she forgot what it was. Her head pounded, she was still too sick to really think clearly, but one idea came to her. Gerard had been absent from the garage. It was possible he was still in his room. Or if he wasn't, she knew he had notes about stuff in Europe. Maybe he had a number she could call for help. Still hungover, feeling cornered in this building, it was the best option Debbie could think of.

Debbie remembered following Simon to Gerard's room earlier. She retraced her steps now and banged on the door. The latch was loose, she remembered now, it didn't quite catch in the frame of the strike plate. Debbie pushed the door open, revealing a dark room. Her hand found the light switch, which illuminated a horror show. She saw congealed blood, a few days old. She saw what looked like maggots. She saw pieces of Gerard. She knew it was Gerard. His head, though separated from the rest of his body, was intact and recognizable. Debbie felt her heart pound in her chest like a jackhammer. Her mouth opened, but no sound came out. Grabbing the doorknob, she pulled the door shut, providing a barrier between herself and the sudden nightmare in the room. She didn't notice GT until he was right beside her.

"Deborah, are you OK?"

"Gerard." Debbie spoke with an effort, backing away from GT. "You-you killed him?"

"No, it was Glasya-Labolas, the author of manslaughter. You helped me vanquish him."

Debbie paused for a moment as the altercation suddenly came back to her. She remembered helping now, she'd stabbed the winged feral dog thing right in the butt. Memories were coming back now. She felt like a grey fog was clearing from her mind. Once more she looked at GT, and that same feeling of warmth and trust came back to her. But she was still on her guard. "So, you did a magic spell on me? Like, without my consent?"

"A ritual and prayer, but I mean that's close enough. I don't want to annoy you by nitpicking. I apologize, but the way you were being mind-controlled I don't know if you'd understand the situation enough to give consent. I told you a lot about the demons and you never remembered what I told you for long. Also, you should know that if these demons succeed, they'll take over the world and kill or enslave everyone. So, while I didn't get your consent, I hope you can understand I have good intentions."

"Why me?"

"I mentioned before how I thought your sexuality might make you less prone to demon influence. Then there's the fact that you've proved yourself capable of fighting some of them, even helping me with a ranking demon of the peerage." GT took a deep breath, clearing his throat. "Also, taking on legions of demons is a heavy burden. I did it once before and barely survived. I'm scared to do it again alone. Having even one person by my side that I could trust, it would really make a difference. You were someone I hoped I might be able to count on."

They were quiet a moment as Debbie looked GT in the eyes. He had shown a moment of fear and doubt, but even as she looked his face became neutral once more. "Who are you, GT?"

"My name is Grant Taylor Whinston, I'm from Wisconsin. My father was a demonologist who forced me to study scripture and demon lore. He raised me to understand and combat demons, and not much else. I hope that answers your question."

"I suppose it does."

"Feel free to ask me anything else." GT said. "I know I can be a little awkward sometimes, say the wrong thing. But I try to be honest and forthright."

"Is the sky really on fire?"

"No, that colour is caused by a layer of demon energy permeating the atmosphere, altering its colour. Duke Astaroth is a demon of the air, so that is where his essence collects as he slowly solidifies his hold on our reality."

"Are my other friends in danger, like will they be killed like Gerard?"

"Not like Gerard, we've neutralized Count Glasya-Labolas. Other legions kill as well, but they act more like mindless animals. Killing to eat, reproduce, or out of reflexive defense. Otherwise, they tend to hold back, submitting to the force of their Duke's will unless directly encountering victims. Glasya-Labolas was the one with the impulsive need to seek out and kill humans for gratuitous pleasure. This need often raises suspicion and makes mind control less effective. Glasya-Labolas has always been a hindrance for that reason. But the Count has similar mind control powers that complement Duke Astaroth's, so the count's presence helps Astaroth take over more quickly. Banishing the count not only slows Astaroth's corrupting influence, but also prevents more immediate murders in the short term. Your friends are still in danger, but Astaroth prefers to operate subtly. The duke solidifies his hold on the world simply by existing in it. All he has to do is to remain on Earth, mind control any humans in the area to keep from being noticed, and let his essence slowly corrupt everything. That corruption gives him a stronger hold in our world, until he cannot be vanquished. Then everyone will suffer."

"Can we stop this?"

"Yes. As I said, I've done it once before."

"How?"

"We fight our way to Astaroth while he is still vulnerable and we send him back to Hell. The legions of minor demons serving beneath him cannot survive without his essence. These legions will also return to Hell, and things will go back to normal. You'll just have to be careful what you tell the authorities afterwards. For obvious reasons they won't accept the truth, especially when all the evidence dissolves back to Hell as the demons die."

"What do we do first?"

"We should take out Astaroth's other lieutenant, Count Malphas. That would weaken Astaroth's position and make the confrontation with him easier. I'm pretty sure I know where Malphas is."

"OK GT, here's how it's going to be: First I need some aspirin and water. Then I need some breakfast. Then I guess we're going demon slaying."

CHAPTER ELEVEN

D ebbie had only a mild headache now. She sat in the passenger seat of GT's Dacia as they drove down the highway outside of town. For a moment the young woman felt a sense of warm nostalgia. She thought of sitting beside her father as they drove together to get some ice cream. It was a happy thought, and she turned to smile at GT. The man began speaking in his emotionless, analytical manner. But there was something reassuring about that too. There was an honesty to him, a sense of solid integrity. On top of that, he was providing useful information.

"So, I believe I mentioned Malphas is currently a Count in Hell's peerage. He was once second to Satan, but there is social mobility amongst the ranks of the peerage. The fact that he now ranks as a lowly count and serves beneath Astaroth, it implies he has lost favour and prestige. As I mentioned earlier, he is affiliated with air demons, and personally takes the shape of a raven. Sometimes he appears as merely the form of the bird, but more commonly he appears as part man and part raven. But as he has not been directly summoned, he'll be covered in the same Pituita Cortex tissue Glasya-Labolas had. In the key of Solomon, he is described as a builder. I'm guessing he is responsible for the construction of the massive hive that hovers over the town."

"Yeah, it's still insane that such a huge object is looming over us."
Debbie said. "That was there the whole time?"

"It was constructed within a week of Astaroth's summoning. He
commands 40 legions of demon minions. Through the planning of
Malphas and the violent discipline of Glasya-Labolas, those legions
worked fast to build it. We can assume Astaroth is there now, working
to expand his power by corrupting the world around him with his
demon essence."

"How far has this corruption spread so far?"

"It grows by the day, but at the moment I would guess his influence
extends through all of the Transylvanian region. That's an area of
perhaps 40,000 square miles and a population of almost 7 million
people he has managed to keep docile. No mean feat, even for a demon
Duke of his power. But mind control is what air demons do. It makes
sense, as they nest in the sky. If they didn't actively mind control the
population, people would be able to see their structures from miles
away."

"Right, but that's not a problem for me anymore, right? That magic
ritual you did made me immune to mind control, didn't it?"

"Astaroth's control, yes. But Malphas can still incorporate illusions
and hallucinations that will appear real to you. You will have complete
control of your mind, but you won't be able to trust what you see with
your own eyes. Your best bet is to avoid snap judgements and think
through whatever is presented before you. Just keep your head and
you'll be able to outwit him."

"I remember studying schizophrenia. I read about this guy who had
auditory hallucinations. He kept a dog and when he had an episode he'd
look to see if his dog reacted to what he was hearing. If the dog didn't
react, he'd know it wasn't real. Do you think that would work with
demon mind control too? Like do demons mind control animals like
humans or would a loyal pet be an asset?"

"That's an excellent question. I honestly don't know. I think something like that could plausibly work, but right now time is against us. It might be worth it to bond with a pet sometime in the future." GT kept his eyes on the road, but Debbie saw him grin. "That was a really good suggestion, Deborah, thank you."

"Now that I'm out of university, I'm getting a dog." Debbie said. "Treat a dog right, and it will be loyal for the rest of its life."

"If only it was so simple with humans. But getting back to Malphas, I know where he is. The hive above us has two supporting struts. They're the only places that allow easy access to the structure. Astaroth kept one lieutenant at each strut until we neutralized Glasya-Labolas. Now he is forced to have Malphas at one and cluster his legion minions around the other. That's how I know where Malphas is."

"So, what's our plan?"

"I'm going to pull over close to the strut with the legions. I'm going to distract them, keep them occupied. This will make it easier for you to strike Malphas directly."

"You want me to fight him alone?" Debbie felt a sudden numbness in her stomach. She had assumed they would confront the demon together.

"We don't want to fight Malphas with legions of minor demons chomping at our heels. I think it makes sense that you take the Count while I distract the legions. With my knowledge, training, and relative experience I'm better suited to handle an army of small Hellish threats. I think it's more likely you will succeed against one foe, even if he is a powerful ranking demon of the peerage." Abruptly GT pulled over, and pulled a folded piece of paper from his pocket. "This is a list of the minion legions, and their weaknesses. In case something happens to me, you will still be prepared to deal with them to some degree. Now I'll get off here, you take the highway East and it will lead you right to

139

the strut. You can easily see it from miles off, you will find it without difficulty."

Debbie took the paper reluctantly (Author's note: List provided in the appendix of this book.) She was still dealing with the idea that she was facing a powerful force of evil alone. "GT, are you sure I can do this?"

"I believe in you." GT said, and the words gave Debbie hope. He pulled a duffle bag from the back seat and took silver from one of the pockets: A stake and a blade. Debbie recognized them from their fight with Glasya-Labolas as once more GT handed them to her. "Remember the count cannot bear Earth's atmosphere without that Pituita Cortex. Peel off even a small area of that tissue, and you'll cause him incredible pain. Just keep cutting him until he melts and you'll know that you've sent him back to his home in Hell. I'm the one who has to get more creative." GT unzipped the duffle bag further, revealing an assortment of objects: Aerosol sprays, pump action sprays, molotov cocktails, grill lighters, silver blades, a bull horn megaphone, and packets of salt. That was just what Debbie could see. "Come pick me up when you're done, and we'll discuss how to deal with Astaroth himself."

Debbie watched GT exit the car, and she took his place behind the wheel. Once more she took out her phone and dialed May's number. Once more there was no answer. Shifting the Dacia into gear, she proceeded down the highway. GT was correct, she didn't have trouble finding the strut. She pulled up beside it, grabbed the silver weapons, and exited the vehicle. As she left the Dacia, she suddenly stepped out into a world of darkness. A familiar voice called out to her as Debbie walked through the gloom. Though her vision was obscured by shadows, she was still able to make out what was before her. A square object to her right, a taller cylindrical object to her left, and a larger figure looming further above. The familiar voice called out to her again.

"You abandoned me." The dim object became clearer to Debbie as she approached. The general shape of a computer monitor, but missing the screen. In place of the missing screen, Liz's head poked through and glared up accusingly. "You knew I was suicidal and you left me to die."

"Oh God, here we go." Debbie had to strain to keep from rolling her eyes. "Where do I even begin? First of all, I didn't abandon you, you left me. Secondly you didn't die. I lurked on your social media for months afterwards. You were fine. For all your talk of suicide and needing help, you sure were resilient without my support in your life. Third, you're obviously not real. The real Liz is in Canada, you demons haven't reached that far. I know you're a hallucination, but I might as well take advantage. Make lemonade out of these lemons."

"What do you mean?" Liz asked. "You should have helped me."

"Since it's not really you, I can freely speak my mind. I want to tell you that you were a horrible friend. You're selfish, you're a burden, you're a leech. You don't give a damn about anyone but yourself. You claim you care about the men you crush on, but all you really care about is how those men make you feel. Meanwhile, how you treated me shows your real character. You used me like a toy and then you cast me aside. People might say that makes me a sucker, but I think it says more about you than it says about me."

"What does it say about me? That my life isn't worth saving? Don't you feel guilty you left me when I was suffering at my lowest point? All the problems I had and you couldn't support me when I needed you the most."

"That really reveals something, doesn't it? People never remember the thousands of times you were there to help them. People only fixate on the one time you let them down. I don't feel a lick of guilt or sympathy for you, Liz. The only regret I have is that I put up with your crap for so damn long! I thought I was being a good friend but now I realize I only enabled your toxic habits. I should have kicked you out of my life years ago. You're a bitch. A stupid, selfish bitch. Shame on me for not seeing that sooner." Abruptly Debbie turned from the woman

in the computer screen and looked up to the figure above. "Were you trying to hurt me with that, Malphas? Because that felt great to finally get that off my chest."

To Debbie's surprise, the looming figure spoke to her in a screeching voice. It was reminiscent of a bird's squawk, but still articulated well enough that Debbie could understand the words. "If you like that, daughter of Eve, I have another gift for you. Look to the pole to your left."

Even as Debbie looked, she saw the image of Andre chained to the pole. The man's arms were stretched above him, his wrists bound to the pole by some kind of rope. His expression was blank, his head lolled to the side. "Another illusion?" Even as Debbie asked, she felt a faint pulse in her left palm. Andre had been such a jackass. One stab of her silver blade in Andre's neck would make his blood spurt out. It would be satisfying, like popping a giant zit.

"He was not respectful." The figure squawked. "It felt so good to leave your friend Liz to kill herself. Now you can do as you wish to another who has wronged you."

Debbie remembered Andre's cocky attitude. She remembered the mocking arrogant way he had spoken to her. It would feel good to put in him in his place. And since it was just an illusion, it didn't really matter anyways. She could beat him, torture him, mutilate him, and it wouldn't matter. It would be as noteworthy as killing a character in a video game. And Andre had been such a pig. What had he said to her again? The words came back to her as she approached the pole. "I remember what he said to me. He had said it in such an arrogant and mocking way, but I remember the words he spoke."

"What does it matter?" The figure asked.

"Andre told me that society cared about him less because he is a man. That if he was hurt or killed, it wouldn't mean as much because society values women more than men. As much of an asshole as he was, as much as I hated him, I knew even then that he had a point." Debbie turned away from the man at the pole. "I don't care if this is an illusion, I'm not even going to pretend to hurt him. Society might not value his life, but I do! I care about the value of a man's life. I'm not the type to laugh at his pain. I refuse to joke about things like male rape and castration. And I certainly won't simulate stabbing him for kicks. Society might find humour or pleasure in that, but I personally don't."

"You would leave your female friend to die. But you will preserve the life of your male enemy?"

"Do you really need me to explain the difference to you?" Debbie gestured from the depiction of Liz to the depiction of Andre. "With Liz I am refusing to enable her fascination with suicide and telling her to grow up. With Andre, I am respecting his life and choosing not to do him any harm. Do you seriously not understand the difference?" Debbie paused for an answer, but all she heard was silence. "GT once told me you demons aren't able to understand the mind of a lesbian woman. I'm beginning to think he's on to something."

Debbie began to approach the looming figure. As she grew closer, the image became clearer. She saw a humanoid figure, covered in some kind of rotting tissue. If it had the shape of a raven mixed with a man, she couldn't tell. What she could tell is that it was an awkward figure trapped in a layer of flesh that limited its mobility. "Wait, you will not harm them, but you will harm me?"

"You're not human, you're a demon. And I'm not even killing you, GT said you're immortal. I'm just kicking you out of Earth and sending you on a trip back to Hell." With that final statement, Debbie lunged forward with her silver. At the last minute the beast dodged, and she merely nicked the exterior tissue with her silver. It was a small gash, but it was enough to elicit a scream from the demon. It recoiled from her, but she continued her attack. She sliced blindly, as the bulky creature withdrew from her assault. Debbie remembered being scared of confronting this creature alone, now she wondered why. A few slashes of her blade reduced it to a whimpering mass at her feet, and as she watched it began to dissolve. Just like Glasya-Labolas, the creature resembled a deflating balloon. As the demon vanished, so too did the shadows begin to dissipate.

Debbie looked around, flush with her victory. As she watched, the computer image of Liz began to dissolve from her sight. Debbie smiled as she turned her attention to Andre's pole. It remained solid. With a sudden feeling of dread, Debbie saw the trap that had been laid out for her. Malphas had actually captured Andre, and set Debbie up to cut his throat. She might have done it too, if she hadn't been so determined to prove a point. It was scary how close Debbie had come to ending the life of an innocent person.

Debbie rushed to the man. It was clear he needed help, but he appeared to be fairly lucid. With her sharp silver blade, Debbie reached up and cut the rope from Andre's wrists. Suddenly released from his bondage, the big man slumped onto Debbie's shoulders. He was heavy, but semi-conscious, and able to stand to a limited degree. Debbie draped the man's arm on her shoulders and half lead, half dragged him to the Dacia. It was a struggle, but she was able to open the door and bundle the taller man into the passenger seat. As she closed the door, she saw how pale Andre looked. This looked serious. Dashing to the driver's side, Debbie took one more look to make sure there was nobody else. All she saw was the strut set into the mountain stone: A solid length of smooth black material, gently sloping up to a structure that loomed overhead. It was an ominous sight, and Debbie felt compelled to leave.

Debbie began driving back down the highway. Her heart was beating like a jackhammer, but she still remembered the plan. She had to pick up GT, then they would go back to town and come up with their next move. As these thoughts crossed her mind, she saw she was speeding 40km over the speed limit. She took a deep breath and pressed on the brake. As the car slowed, she saw GT running up to her. He pulled open the door and leapt into the backseat behind her. "Drive! Quickly!" GT shouted, slamming the car door behind him. As he did so, Debbie heard a smattering of sound against the side of the car. She couldn't see what was hitting them, but it sounded rather like hail smacking against the lower side of the car doors. Debbie decided she didn't want to know. She would trust GT's judgement. Pressing her foot on the accelerator, she sped back into town.

CHAPTER TWELVE

"Andre is hurt, I don't know how badly." Debbie said, keeping her eyes on the road.

"Let's see." Behind her, GT reached forward and felt Andre's neck and forehead. She heard Andre moan as GT examined him. "His pulse is solid, he's semi-conscious. He's pale. Based on what I know of Astaroth's legions, I'd say he was drugged by an Alantus Anguis."

"What's that?"

"It's a snake with feathered wings and a venomous narcotic in its bite. It's listed on that paper I gave you."

"I'm sorry, I've been too busy to read it."

"The venom in the bite tends to subdue the prey, as the Alantus Anguis devours its victims whole and living. It can be lethal, but someone of Andre's bodyweight should be fine. In fact, he already seems to be recovering. I suggest he be monitored for a few hours, to see if this goes away. If symptoms persist beyond three hours, then we might want to risk taking him to the hospital."

"Why is that a risk?"

"It will involve the authorities. I mentioned before how difficult it is to speak about demons to the police. They will want answers we can't give. Time is working against us."

"What do you mean?"

"Astaroth cannot spread his essence, mind control the populace, and keep his legions in line all at the same time. That is why he employs lesser members of the peerage. With both of his Lieutenants sent back to Hell, the legions will begin to operate independently. They will leave the hive and prowl like animals. Mainly they will want nourishment, and they prefer to eat human beings. The good news is this will make Astaroth more vulnerable as his guards will leave the hive. The bad news is the longer we delay the more people could die."

"How do we deal with legions of demons?" Debbie asked. They were nearing the outskirts of the town now.

"We don't have to. If we vanquish Astaroth, everything demonic goes back to Hell with him. So, we just have to take him out. That does present another problem though. The hive is constructed from demonic materials, and it will dissolve quickly just like everything else. That will leave us suspended high above the mountains, ready to fall back to the earth. So, we'd need to kill Astaroth and head back to solid ground at full speed."

"I looked at the struts. They're too narrow for this car, but I could get up them on my motorcycle."

"I've never driven a motorcycle."

"We can share mine." Debbie flashed GT a smirk. "You won't feel emasculated sitting on the back of my bike, will you?"

"Of course not, why would I care about that?"

"Cool, we have a plan then. Let's drop Andre back at the garage. I'm sure some of my friends will be there, I'll ask them to take care of him. We'll pick up my bike and drive back up the mountains." Coming up to the garage, Debbie parked the car and turned to Andre. The man was looking better, already he looked more alert. "Andre, how are you feeling now?"

"I- I don't know. I feel funny." Andre said, speaking coherently now. Debbie got out of the car and rushed to the passenger side. Andre seemed to be able to completely stand on his own. That, combined with the fact that he was able to speak suggested GT was right about his recovery. Andre still seemed confused, and Debbie had to take him by the hand and lead him into the garage. As she looked back, she locked eyes with GT. He would stand guard, just in case.

Debbie and Andre entered the garage to a chorus of relieved sighs. Emmanuel, Trixie, and Simon were there, and appeared to have been worried about both of them. Emmanuel spoke first. "Debbie, you found him! What happened? Where was he? Andre, are you alright, man?"

"I found him up in the mountains." Debbie said. It was technically true. "He might have done some kind of drug up there. He seems a little out of it."

"Andre, did you take something exotic and not share with your bro?" Emmanuel spoke in a teasing tone, but he still looked worried. They guided Andre to a chair by a tool bench and had him sit down.

"We all party sometimes, I don't want to be a narc about it. He already seems to be getting better." Debbie remembered what GT had said about hospital delays. If they took Andre to the hospital instead of her, that would be ideal. But she had to choose her words carefully.

"It might be nice if you looked after him just in case, Manny. If he still seems out of it after a while, you might want to take him to the hospital. Maybe you could look out for him too, Trixie, if it's not a problem. I'd watch him myself, but I have something really important I promised to take care of."

"You already brought him back. You're a hero, girl!" Trixie said. "We'll watch Andre, ain't the first time I've done some babysitting."

"I knew you guys would understand." Debbie headed to her bike, taking out her cell phone as she did so. Once more she dialed May. This time, someone picked up.

"I know your number, stop calling this phone." Debbie recognized the voice, it was May's father.

"Look I don't mean to- I just wanted to know, is May OK?"

"She is fine, you stop calling now." The man terminated the call before Debbie was able to speak any further. Debbie stared at the phone in frustration, tempted to throw it across the garage. Instead, she slipped her cell back into her pocket and went to her bike. Simon came to her side as she oriented the Kawasaki.

"Debbie, are you alright?"

"Simon, I need a favour." Debbie said, as she did a last minute check of her vehicle. "I have to do a thing with GT. It's really important. While I'm gone can you maybe try to look in on May. I haven't been able to reach her on the phone, and I'm scared something bad might happen to her."

"GT, that weirdo we talked to in the bar?" Debbie nodded, and Simon shrugged. "Well, if you want me to, I'll look in on May, no problem. But are you sure you want to spend time with that creep?"

"Look, I know it's weird and I can't really explain it. There's something about GT that makes me trust him. There's a warmth to him, an honesty, an integrity that you see when you look into his eyes. So, when he asks me to do him a favour, I trust him." As Debbie spoke, she saw that her Kawasaki was ready to go.

"Debbie?"

"Yes?" Debbie looked up from her bike and looked Simon in the eyes.

"You realize that's how people feel when they talk to you, right? You have a kind of warmth and honesty as well."

It was a simple compliment, but in that moment, it meant a lot to Debbie. She felt her cheeks flush slightly, and she gave Simon a friendly punch on the shoulder. "Thanks bro, that's really nice to hear. You're a good friend, a really good guy." With that statement, Debbie revved the engine of her motorcycle and drove out of the garage. GT was still waiting outside, and hopped on the bike behind her. Together they rode out of the town and back into the mountains.

Debbie had driven her bike through these mountains repeatedly with May. But now, with her vision cleared of demon illusions, she saw the mountain forests in a new light. Trees had bulky nests swarming with things too big to be insects. Just off the road, clusters of red snakes slithered in a dense swarm, appearing more like a single entity than a group of individual animals. Further off from the highway she saw what appeared to be shadows of figures too twisted to be human. Even the road in front of her seemed to be gradually warping and changing. It was subtle, but it made Debbie think of something Simon had told her about old movies. The film techniques of Germans like Fritz Lang, creating a visual style called "German Expressionism." An abstract representation of what existed in the real world through an impossible exaggeration of reality. Debbie thought of that now as she saw reality warp ever so slightly under the influence of a Duke of Hell. Behind Debbie, GT sensed her hesitation and yelled at her over the rush of the

wind and the roar of her bike's engine. "Don't dwell on these things. Just focus on our goal." It was good advice, and Debbie sped on until they reached the strut. Adjusting for the upward angle, Debbie slowed her speed to orient her bike. Then she revved the engine once more and they began their ascent to the nest. The strut was a straight climb upwards, but upon reaching the interior of the bizarre alien structure above, things changed.

It was similar to Debbie's encounter with Malphas. One moment it was a bright August afternoon. The light was tainted by orange demonic essence, but it was still easy to see. Upon entering the Hive, Debbie and GT found themselves cloaked in inky black shadows. It was an unnatural darkness, as the structure of the Hive was not completely enclosed. Though he was only a few feet away, Debbie had to squint to see GT. "Just stab some silver into him if you can." GT said. "I'll need to pray over Astaroth and conduct a ritual to completely vanquish him. But hurting him with our silver blades will make things a lot easier. We just have to find him."

"Find me? Are you implying I would hide from such as you?" A voice reverberated in the darkness. It was a low, arrogant sounding voice. At once Debbie thought of Tom Cruise from the film "Interview with the Vampire." Take Tom Cruise's portrayal of Lestat, make his voice deeper, and allow it to reverberate in an unnatural way. That was the voice she now heard.

"Astaroth!" GT cried out. His voice trembled slightly, but there was a firm resolve to it as well. "Once you were considered a peer to Lucifer himself. One of the first of the hierarchy that ruled Hell. But now you are merely a Duke of the peerage! That not only ranks you as an inferior to Lucifer, but also as an inferior to all Nine Kings of Hell! What disgrace caused you to lose face amongst the peerage? Was it your failure to seduce Saint Bartholomew?"

"You wish to challenge me, mortal?" Astaroth's voice echoed in the darkness. "Are you really in a position to do so? How solid a foundation do you stand upon, Whinston? You have devoted your entire life to opposing demons like me. Have you ever asked yourself why you have done so? Is it because your father told you to? Your father, the same man who forced you to learn demon lore under the threat of corporal punishment? The man who deprived you of a real childhood? The man who raised you to lack any accredited education or relevant life skills, so that you would waste your youth doing nothing but opposing us. Is it really worth risking your life to fight for the memory of a man like that? Or are you driven forward by the constant urgings of my peer, the demon Duke Zaleos? Does it not bother you that one of your only allies in your lifelong struggle is nothing more than another demon of Hell?"

The dark shadows seemed to swallow GT completely. Not only visually, but audibly as well. If GT replied to the demon Duke, Debbie didn't hear it. The young woman cried out in the darkness. "GT, I'm your ally too."

"Ah, the dyke abomination from half a world away. The woman who wasted four years on a useless degree, and forms her identity around her sexuality because she has no real direction in her life."

"No, that's not- I mean-." The words hit Debbie hard. She didn't want to admit it, but there was truth to what the demon had said. "How do you know that?"

"Oh, I know. I see right through you. Nobody looks deeper into the minds of a mortal than Astaroth. I warp the very fabric of your reality, dominate your perception, and twist your mind like taffy. But we're not talking about me, we're talking about you. The way you have failed in your life. You've wasted your youth, wasted your talents, wasted the opportunities that you never deserved in the first place."

"I'm still young. Still trying to figure things out. That's not a bad thing."

"I've watched humanity evolve throughout the centuries. The greatest of you knew your purpose even as children. Figuring things out is just an excuse for weakness."

"I don't care what other people have done." In the darkness, Debbie still had the silver weapons GT had given her. She clutched them close now, trying to get angry. Anger would drive out her uncertainty. It would make her brave. "I'm me, and I will live my own life by my own rules. I will take as long as I want to figure my life out, and nobody can tell me otherwise."

"Oh yes, you're a strong woman who doesn't need a man." Astaroth said, his voice full of mockery. "That is except for your father. The man who has worked his fingers to the bone to provide for you. The man who paid for your trip through Europe. The man who also paid for your entire University degree. A useless degree, remember. You could have studied anything, but you squandered your father's money on a degree that you know is worth nothing. How long did your father toil to provide you with the funds for your education? He worked so hard, and hoped you would pursue something worth his investment. And what did you choose to do?"

The words caught in Debbie's throat as she struggled to respond. Once again there was real truth to what the demon was saying. She had worked part time during the summers, but her father had paid for the lion's share of her expenses. She thought about the last four years she had spent on Psychology, studies she barely remembered. What would have happened if she had spent her time on something more marketable, like an engineering degree? It would have been so much harder. She pictured herself spending endless hours memorizing the most boring concepts. Taking on a responsibility beyond her abilities, complicated math that she could barely understand. But at the same time, she pictured how proud her father would have been. And how many more opportunities she could enjoy, now that her studies were complete. Four years of a degree her father had paid for. Four years she could have spent so much more wisely. Debbie forced herself to speak into the darkness. "I chose something that interested me. Yeah, it wasn't the most marketable degree, but- I mean- money isn't everything."

"You exist in a capitalist system. I would say money matters a great deal. What of your mother. Your last memory of her is of her hands around your throat. She hated you, she was so disappointed in you. You think it was because she's a closed minded conservative. Did it ever occur to you that she had other reasons to be frustrated with her only child? Was it only bigotry that made her lash out, or did you completely fail her as a daughter?"

That had been one of the most traumatic experiences of Debbie's life: Her own mother's hands around her neck. The strangulation itself hadn't been so bad, physically Debbie had endured worse. But the fact that it was her own mother choking her, cursing her with an expression of hatred. That was what made it such a painful memory. It was a horrible moment, one that was burned into Debbie's mind with perfect clarity. But she also remembered what had happened after that moment. "My mother apologized to me for lashing out. It was strained, and only partially sincere. But why would she apologize if I was in the wrong?" In the moment it felt like a tenuous defense, but she felt there was some truth to it. "If I am at fault, then she wouldn't apologize to me. She would have expected me to apologize to her. But that's not what happened."

"That's pathetic. You're a horrible person and you know it."

"I'm pathetic? You're the one hiding in the shadows!"

"And yet you're the one hiding from the truth."

"You're a demon, you probably don't even understand concepts like truth. Or any noble ideas like justice, compassion, or love."

"You claim to be an expert on love, Miss Ryans?"

"Hey at least I have a girlfriend. I somehow doubt you've had healthy relationships."

"Oh, that's right, your lover. How long have you known her now? Has it been one whole week or two?"

"Time doesn't mean anything. Love can bloom in an instant and last a lifetime."

"Love that lasts a lifetime." Astaroth laughed in the darkness. "Tell me about your lover. What are her hopes and dreams? What hobbies does she have? Who are her role models and inspirations? How about her family history or her specific religious beliefs? What do you even know about her at all?"

"Well, I mean-." Debbie faltered. The first thing that came to mind was what May had shared about her anxiety, trauma, and family problems. But Debbie wasn't about to discuss that with a demon. She thought harder as it occurred to her how little she actually knew about her girlfriend. She hadn't thought about it before, how they had spent their time together. Mostly Debbie had talked and May had listened. She had been so wrapped up in the happiness of the moment that she hadn't thought about how such a relationship would last in the long term. But as these thoughts went through her mind, she could feel a stubborn anger override her hesitation. She refused to let Astaroth win this argument. "She likes to go hiking and biking with me. She's a good listener and likes it when I tell her stuff."

"Have you ever considered that she doesn't really like those activities? That perhaps she merely endured them because they're things you enjoy? She told you before that she has anxiety, that oftentimes she feels safest in her house. Do you really think being outside in public all the time is ideal for her?"

"Sure, it's healthy to get out of the house." Even as she said this, Debbie's mind flashed back to a Psychology class. She recalled descriptions of anxiety, how debilitating such a condition could be. How it could make one prone to attacks of emotional anguish very similar to physical pain. Had May risked enduring an experience like that, just to be accommodating? "She said she felt safe around me."

"I'm sure she'd never lie to placate you in any way. Especially when you've known each other for so long. Certainly, lying to be polite and avoid a fuss is something that is never done."

"No, she- I don't think she'd do that. I know her."

"Oh of course you do." Astaroth paused for a moment. "Remind me, Deborah Lauren Ryans, what's May's full name again?"

"It's Maia-um." Debbie had to struggle to think for a moment. "Her last name starts with a P, it's uh- wait it's Popescu. Maia Popescu."

"That took you long enough. But that's not her full name. What's her middle name?"

"I-." Debbie clenched her fist in frustration. That must have come up at some point. She even remembered May putting her full name on a form when they had gone to the hospital. She had been distracted at the time, she remembered watching May write something down. But at the moment, Debbie's mind was blank.

"Do you need a hint?" The demon asked. "Rather hilarious that I know this information and you don't."

"Shut up, this is stupid anyways." Sudden anger pushed the doubt from Debbie's mind. "I'm here to fight, not have you judge my love life. Quit hiding and face me!"

"I'm not hiding, I just think I am more than a mortal like you can bear."

"Don't do me any favours, just show yourself!"

"The sight of me has driven mortals mad. Are you certain you can take it, defective daughter of Eve?"

"Do I stutter? Cut the crap and face me directly." As Debbie spoke, she saw the shadows begin to part. She had to blink as her eyes adjusted to what appeared to be a bright orange light. Beyond that light she saw a figure. That figure defied her understanding of reality, and she had to strain to even comprehend it. It seemed larger at the bottom, she could process that much. At the bottom was a darkness with gleams of light glowing through what looked like split seams. But the darkness had a shape to it, like the imposing dragons in the fairy tales she had read of as a little girl. Something born of a primal fear she hadn't experienced in over a decade. In the middle of this shadowy form, seemingly fused to the arch of its spine, she saw the figure of a man. Only the man was thicker, taller, and seemed to be composed of a bright orange ember that flickered as Debbie watched. The glowing orange figure, fused to the dragon of shadow, had an arm that stretched from him at an impossible length. That arm transitioned to a serpent, though Debbie could not tell exactly where the arm ended and the serpent began. All she could say is that the serpent seemed the most real. While the dragon below was a shadow punctuated with streaks of white light, and the man above was a being of burning orange energy, the serpent was just a normal giant snake. And that snake was coiling to strike Debbie even as she watched. Abruptly, the snake lunged.

Debbie acted on reflex. Her mind was still numb from Astaroth's words. Perhaps she had wasted her entire adult life so far. Perhaps she had failed her parents, failed May and failed herself. Perhaps she had relied on her sexuality too much when forming her own identity. Perhaps she was still wasting time aimlessly touring Europe. But in the heat of the moment, with a recognized predator snake striking at her, none of that mattered. Her instincts mattered, her need for survival. She jumped back, as the massive serpent's fangs just missed beneath her. The body of the monster clipped her, and she tumbled head over

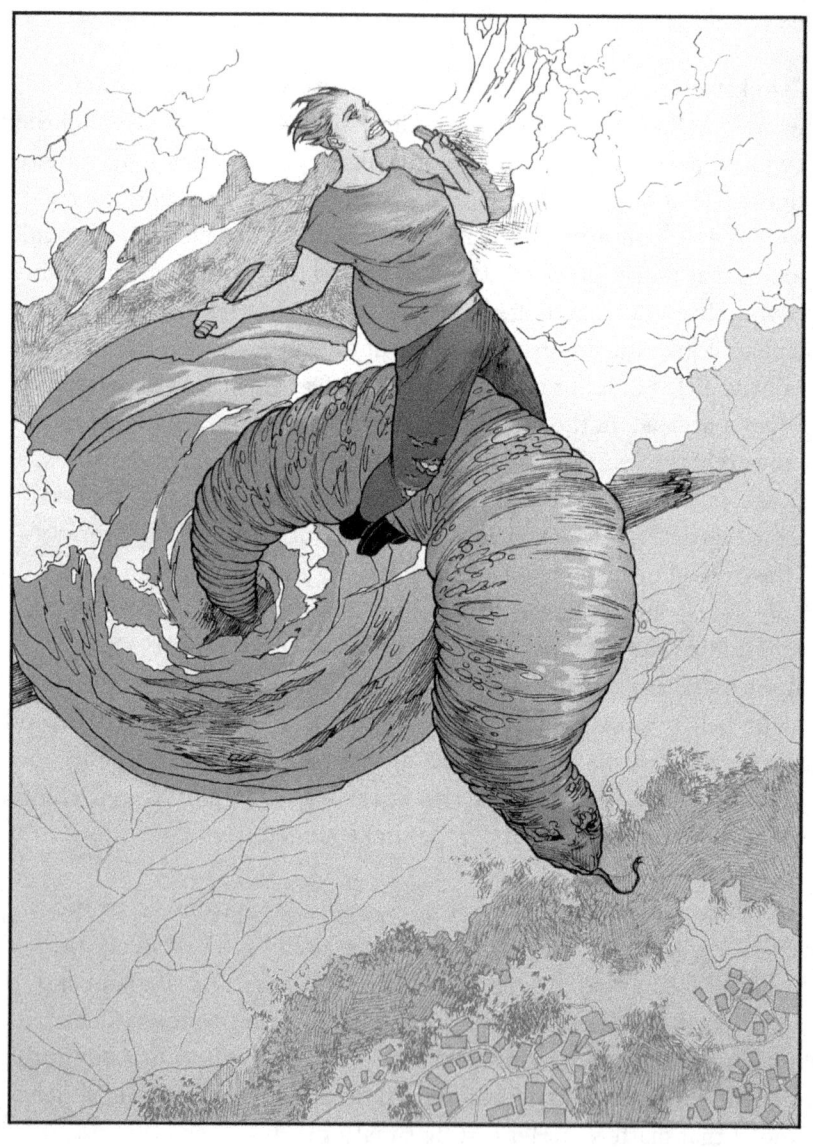

heels from the force of the blow. The snake was bigger around than a trash can, and had moved with terrifying speed. Though the snake had missed with its fangs, Debbie was knocked backward by the momentum of the lunge. Abruptly the shadows fell away, as she found herself dangling high in the orange sky. Beneath her, the snake's torso twisted and thrashed. And further below, at least 3000 feet below, she saw the town and surrounding farmland. It was a long drop, and Debbie was struggling to keep her balance sprawled on top of the giant snake. She'd like to think her job as a roofer had cured her of any fear of heights. But this was much higher up, on a surface that was much more precarious. She still remembered something from that job, though. She needed to establish an anchor point. Her hands still clutched silver weapons, and she stabbed the pointed stake down into the scaley flesh beneath her. The snake recoiled on contact, pulling itself back into the hive, with Debbie still anchored on top of it. As they reentered the gloom, Debbie saw the shadows shimmer and begin to part. She also saw GT, lunging at the shadowy demon with his own silver weapons.

"Well struck, Astaroth is vulnerable!" GT cried. "Hit him while you still can." Once more Debbie acted on instinct. The snake had twisted the stake from her grip, but she still had her blade. She slashed with the weapon, feeling resistance as it cut through something in the darkness. Around her, Debbie felt the world shiver and quake. Abruptly the shadows fell away, and GT was in front of her, straddling a smaller being. The demon still had the same general shape. She saw what appeared to be a dragon beneath, a man fused to it above, and a snake fused to that man's arm. But it all seemed smaller now, more contained. More understandable. GT was doing something to the creature. He moved quickly, competently, efficiently. She heard him quote the Bible, she saw him breath on the demon with exaggerated puffs of air. She saw him apply salt. Finally, she heard GT conclude his ritual: "In Saint Michael's name, Duke Astaroth, you are condemned to Hell. Depart ye cursed into everlasting fire, prepared for the devil and his angels."

What happened next was a blur for Debbie. She remembered the ground beginning to shake beneath her feet. She remembered GT grabbing her roughly by the hand and guiding her to her motorcycle. They had gotten on, and she had started the engine. Things became clearer as she drove the bike forward. She saw the strut, even as the world seemed to quake around her. She aimed for it, suddenly feeling like she was threading a needle. It was a bumpy ride, but she was used to her bike by this point. She drove them both smoothly down the strut and onto a plateau of the Carpathian Mountains. She coasted the Kawasaki to a standstill, and became aware of GT rising from the seat behind her. Together they turned back and looked at the hive that had loomed over the town above them. Already it appeared to dissolve. She saw pieces of the structure fall off, only to disappear before they hit the town below. The solid black structure was evaporating into the blue sky above. Debbie had to blink a moment, and double check. It was true, once more the sky was blue. The Hellish orange glow was gone. Debbie checked her phone, and cried out in surprise. She turned to GT. "We were up there for 18 hours? It felt like twenty minutes tops."

"Demons can alter reality around them. You'll see space and time warp to some degree if you get close to them. As I've said before, vanquishing them is not easy and there's always a cost."

"Did we get him? Is it over?"

"Basically yes. The only thing that bothers me is who summoned Astaroth in the first place. Demons of Hell can only come to Earth through the cooperation of human beings." GT thought for a moment. "But I suppose we've taken care of the immediate problem. There will be some minor issues with the police to clear up. They'll want to know about Gerard, among other things. We'll need to report his death and make sure we're not blamed for it. We'll have to be careful not to mention demons to them. As long as we're smart, we'll be able to walk away from this."

"I already feel completely drained. I can't even think about Gerard right now. Can you please give me one day to process all this and get myself back to reality." Debbie saw GT shrug beside her. "At the very least, I need to check on my girlfriend, May."

CHAPTER THIRTEEN

At GT's request, Debbie rode back down the mountain and dropped him off at the outskirts of town. Her next stop was the garage, which she found to be empty. Debbie took out her cell phone. Her first instinct was to try calling May again. Once more her call went to voice mail. That option exhausted, she dialed Simon. He picked up immediately. Debbie still felt a little anxious from her recent ordeal, but she forced herself to remain calm. "Hi Simon, what did I miss?"

"Hey Debbie. We ended up taking Andre to the hospital, Trixie and Manny are still with him. He's doing fine, but they wanted to keep him a little longer. Apparently whatever drug he had in his system, it's something the doctors have never seen before."

Debbie thought about what GT had said earlier, how all demon material would vanish with Astaroth. She wondered how that would affect the medical tests. They'd had 18 hours to work with whatever was in Andre's system, but it would be gone now. "Well, glad everyone is OK. Did you get a chance to see May?"

"Yeah, uh, about that. I don't want to upset you, but um-."

"Just be honest, Simon." Debbie steeled herself for bad news. "You won't upset me, I promise."

"I wasn't able to talk to her, but I followed her. I mean, it felt a little creepy, but I figured it was really important to you. I saw her kiss this guy on the lips."

"Did you say a guy? A man?"

"Yeah, I thought that would bother you. I waited till she left and introduced myself to him. He said his name is Florin Muller."

"What?! She's hooking up with him?"

"Don't shoot the messenger, OK Debbie?"

"She's seeing him behind my back? That creep, of all people?! I can offer her so much more than that worthless-." Debbie felt the words catch in her throat as her face flushed with anger.

"I thought you told me that was a juvenile way to look at relationships."

Abruptly Debbie had to restrain herself from smashing her phone on the pavement. Simon might be correct, but she wasn't in the mood to hear it. She took a deep breath and forced herself to remain calm. She reminded herself that Simon was her friend. "Simon, thank you for giving me this information. It's made me extremely angry, too angry to talk right now. But thank you anyways. I need to go, I'm sorry."

"Yeah, I understa-." Debbie terminated the call as Simon was speaking. Her teeth were clenched in anger. Slipping the phone back in her pocket, she revved her bike and tore out of the garage. She knew the bar Florin worked at. She rode out of the town, down the highway. It was a fair distance to that bar, but the time did nothing to dull her rage. All she could think of was her picnic with May. How the young woman had struggled to explain one of the worst experiences of her life. How could May even consider being with a man like that? Ahead of her she saw the bar, lined with trees she had hidden in earlier, with a blade in her hand. Debbie parked her bike and approached the bar. She was going to confront Florin Muller. She was going to get answers.

It was still early in the evening when she entered. She saw Florin arranging the stools at the end of the bar. They were alone, but he heard her come in. He spoke to her in Romanian, then again in English. "Hello, we just open. You want drink?"

"I'm not here to drink, I'm here to talk to you, Florin Muller."

"Yes, I speak some English, I can talk. Nice to meet you, what is your name?" The young man walked towards Debbie, his hand outstretched.

"I am not shaking your hand!" Debbie shouted. The anger of her words made Florin recoil. He looked at the young woman in silence for a moment as Debbie glared back at him. They were interrupted by a woman emerging from behind the bar. Debbie recognized May, and felt some of her fury dissipate. Even now, as flustered as she was, the presence of May was enough to cool some of Debbie's anger. May spoke to Florin in Romanian, and the young man returned to the bar, nodding in understanding. Then May turned her attention to Debbie, motioning her out of the bar. Debbie couldn't help but see fear in May's eyes, as they walked outside together. "May, what the hell is going on?"

Once they were outside, May spoke with measured calm. "I don't want to hurt you. I want to be kind and polite to you. I choose Florin. We are both adults, I am sure you can understand. It was nice to be with you, you were wonderful. But I am sorry, it is over now. Please forgive me if I hurt you."

"I don't understand." Debbie suddenly felt numb. She heard May's words, she understood them. She was being shot down, Debbie processed that much. Pain would come later, but right now she only felt confusion. "Why? Why is this happening? Why him?"

"I look on internet. I see term called 'bicurious phase.' That is what you were, Deborah. You were my bicurious phase. I had it briefly, because I am young woman. But it passed over now. It is done. I am sorry." May spoke the words robotically, without emotion. She did not meet Debbie's eyes.

"No May, that's utter nonsense. You made me a scrapbook."

"I told you already I do that often. It is a habit I have. It means nothing."

"I thought you were being coy when you said that. I really cared about you, May. I saw a real future with you."

"Yes, well, I do not see future with you." May still spoke robotically, her eyes still cast to the side.

"May, I don't believe you. Look me in the eyes, tell me the truth!" Debbie felt the numbness inside of her being pushed out by anger. May was lying to her, Debbie focused on that fact. That was wrong, it was wrong for May to lie to her. May was free to date whoever she wanted to. May could dump Debbie if she wanted to. May could tear Debbie's heart out and stomp on it if she wanted to. All of that was something Debbie had to deal with, as a mature adult. But it was wrong for May to lie. Debbie clung to that one fact in the midst of this emotional hurricane. She could respect May's decision, but she would not respect her lying.

"You should already know!" Abruptly May locked eyes with Debbie, and Debbie saw pain and anger in those eyes. "I come here to talk to my old boyfriend. I come out and see you with a knife in your hands. I see your eyes, you have killer's eyes. It show me you were always criminal. Always riding your dangerous bike, sneaking me out behind my father's back. Putting me in situation where I have to go to hospital."

"No, that's not true."

"Seeing you that night finally help me to open my eyes. You were going to kill Florin. It was the most scary thing I see in my life. Why do you think I hug you that night?"

"I thought- I thought you did it because you loved me?" The words became a question as Debbie thought back to that night.

"I do it because I was so scared you would kill an innocent man. The only thing I think of was to hold you back with my arms. I make you calm down from your killer passion."

"An innocent man?" Another detail Debbie grasped at. This was a horrible experience, a tumultuous ride. But she could grasp at this one fact. Florin was not innocent. "You call Florin innocent? How can you say that?!"

"I say he is innocent. I say that, because I know my life better than you do. I know what I see. Also, one thing I see is that you are willing to be a killer. I will not date a killer."

"That's not me." The words felt weak and impotent as they left Debbie's mouth, but she didn't know what else to say.

"Just leave. I am sorry if I hurt you but I make my choice. Don't talk to me anymore. Don't phone me. Just leave."

With those final words, May turned away from Debbie and went back into the bar. Debbie watched her go. She watched May walk to Florin, and she saw the two of them kiss. That last image was too much. Debbie turned away, and walked back to her bike. She straddled the Kawasaki, and revved the engine. For motorcycles, Japanese models tend to be quieter and more efficient than American models, like a Harley Davidson. Still Debbie did her best to rev the engine of her bike several times, hoping the noise would somehow distract May. It was juvenile, it was futile, and Debbie knew it. Turning away from the bar, Debbie drove her bike back onto the highway.

How Debbie felt at this moment was difficult to describe. Her anger had been reduced to a dull roar in the back of her mind. May's words had caused a numbness to creep over her rage, causing her to feel slightly detached. But as she rode her Kawasaki down the highway, Debbie felt the cool summer wind blow through her hair. It was a beautiful day, and she was in small town Romania in August. The countryside was still breathtaking. Debbie could shift her focus to the environment around her, to get her mind off of what she'd just gone through. She saw a country road and turned onto it. There were new adventures around every corner if one knew where to look. She was still a young woman on a vacation in Eastern Europe.

Debbie rode her motorcycle down the smaller road as it turned to gravel beneath her. All around her she saw green, except for some distant farmland, where she saw wheat turning gold. Above her, in the early evening, she saw blue sky. In that blue sky she saw the sun only beginning its descent to the Carpathian Mountains. Romania had some beautiful areas to explore. As hurt as Debbie was, she couldn't help but marvel at the simple miracles that nature offered on a daily basis. She remembered a statement she had heard once from a documentary called "Zen - The Best of Alan Watts." She couldn't remember the exact words, but she remembered the concept Alan Watts had presented: "Two brothers wanted to find themselves. The rich brother took a trip around the world. The poor brother took a trip around his garden. Both were enriched by their experiences." The point was that beauty could be found in the grandest and simplest displays of what the world had to offer. One just had to be willing to look. Debbie was willing to look now. She drove her Kawasaki further into the Romanian countryside.

It was a night the young woman would never forget. She saw a dairy farm where people cared for their cows. She parked her bike at the outskirts of the farm, and approached the people as they milked those cows. The farmhands looked at her with confusion and apprehension, but Debbie's warm smile and friendly demeanor was enough to put them at ease. They didn't speak English, but they let her walk up to

the cows and pet them. They were docile animals, they remained calm when Debbie approached them. She smiled at the farmhands, and one of them bumped fists with her. As she walked away from the animals and got back on her bike, Debbie thought briefly about how much May would have enjoyed such an experience. They had gone to a farm together before. She pushed that thought from her mind as she drove further down the highway.

Debbie rode her bike over a bridge that crested a wide stream. The young woman parked her vehicle and stood at the stream for a moment. The sun was just cresting the Carpathian Mountains, but it still shone brightly. Debbie saw reflections of the sun on the water, and she took some stones from the bank and skipped them along the water's surface. Skipping rocks was something she had done with her father. She remembered how he had told her to look for flatter rocks, that would skip better along the surface. Looking along the bank of the stream, she found a few that would work. She managed to skip the rocks with some degree of proficiency. Mainly two skips, sometimes three skips, at one point she managed four skips. That was enough of a personal accomplishment as far as Debbie was concerned. For a moment she wondered how May would have done at such a game. She imagined May wouldn't have been very good. May would have looked to Debbie for guidance and Debbie would have been happy to give it. It would have been really cute to teach May that simple game. Once again Debbie pushed the idea from her mind. She got back on her bike and rode further down the highway.

The sun set as Debbie continued her ride. She paused at a Rompetrol service station to fill her tank. Debbie had to remind herself that it was called petrol in Europe, not gas. She remembered a funny quote from an Englishmen she'd read on the internet: "Why do you yanks call petrol gas when it's clearly a liquid." She wondered how May would have interpreted such a joke, with her limited grasp of English. Once more, Debbie had to force such a question from her mind. She drove away from the service station as she saw stars begin to light up the night sky. As she drove into the Carpathian Mountains, she couldn't help but find her gaze drifting upwards.

The stars really were beautiful. In Romania, up in the mountains, away from light pollution, Debbie had time to really look up at those stars. It was a breathtaking experience. The sky looked so dark and against such a dark background, the stars shone with radiant clarity. Debbie parked her bike, and simply leaned against it, looking up at the summer sky. The stars seemed to shimmer as she gazed up at them. Her whole life she knew there were stars in the sky, but how often had she really taken the time to stop and look at them? Out in the country dark, they were more vibrant and bright than she'd ever seen them before. At this moment she wished she had paid more attention to the study of astronomy. She recognized the big dipper, and thought she could find the north star. Beyond that all she saw was a twinkling wonder of jewels against a velvet black. But that was OK, it was still a magical experience. One that would stay with Debbie as she continued riding down the highway.

Just riding her motorcycle down the highway was a liberating adventure. In the dead of night, in the outskirts of Romania, tearing down the highway on a reliable Kawasaki. That was an experience. She saw other cars on the road, but they were infrequent. A flash of high-beams, then they were gone. If Debbie let her imagination wander, she could pretend the whole world was hers to explore. The beam of her Kawasaki lit up the highway, and above her the stars in the sky lit up the night. In the back of her mind she still felt a twinge of emotional pain, but she could push that away as she embraced the moment. She was a young woman, fresh out of college, exploring the wonders of Europe. How could she feel sad when she saw such limitless possibilities before her? She had been intimidated by that freedom before, but now it was something she was ready to embrace.

Debbie spent the whole night exploring the backroads of Romania. Ahead of her she saw the sky begin to brighten, she saw the sun crest the horizon, and she was reminded of her promise to GT. Before going to visit him, she stopped one more time. May's scrapbook was still in her saddlebags. Debbie took it out and examined it again. She remembered going over the book, and being touched by its sentimentality. But looking at it now, all she saw was scraps of garbage and junk, taped to a cheap object that could be bought at any number of local stores. Without May to give these items meaning, the scrapbook was a waste of space. Debbie had no reason to carry it with her anymore. She should just throw it into the woods and make a clean break. But even as that thought crossed her mind, Debbie carefully closed the book and placed it back in her saddlebag. As painful as the past was, it was still a part of her. At one point May had given her that book as a gift of love. For the sake of that one moment, Debbie would hold onto that scrapbook. She got back on her bike and headed off to keep her appointment.

Debbie found GT not far from where she had dropped him off, just on the outskirts of town. She saw the young man's face light up as she parked her bike beside him. "It looks like the harm from the demons was minimal. Some buildings were damaged, there were higher admissions to the hospital. But there were fewer deaths than I'd anticipated."

"Right, yeah, hi GT." Now that Debbie was with a native English speaker, she felt some of the night's enchantment fade. She felt like she was leaving the magic of a faraway European wonderland and returning to reality. "Something kinda crazy happened to me."

"What's wrong? Are you OK?"

"Physically? Yes, I'm fine." Debbie said. "It's just emotionally, I feel like... I want to talk to someone. May dumped me. And she did it in a really crappy and horrible way."

"I'm sorry to hear that." GT said. The words were perfunctory, but Debbie wanted to believe he was sincere.

"It's so completely unfair." The more Debbie spoke, the more she began to grasp the reality of what had happened. "I mean it's just blow after blow after blow. Number one, I get dumped totally out of the blue. Number two, my lesbian girlfriend dumps me for a man. That's always an extra kick in the guts. But number three, she dumps me for a man like Florin Muller. The guy is a horrible, vile, evil piece of crap. I would rather she went with anyone but him. I mean, he's-." Suddenly a thought came to Debbie. "GT, was May mind controlled by those demons in any way?"

"Just a moment, I'll ask." Abruptly GT turned away from Debbie. The young woman watched as GT walked down the highway. He walked a distance of perhaps twenty yards, and appeared to be muttering to himself. Then just as abruptly, the young man turned and walked back to Debbie. "No, I don't think she was."

"Are you sure?"

"Based on how eager Zaleos was to speak to me about this, and the way he spoke to me, yes I'm pretty sure."

"What do you mean? How did he speak to you? What were his exact words?"

"His exact words were: 'Oh no, she can't blame that on us. May betrayed her of her own free will. Love is suffering for you mortals, is it not?' And after saying that, he laughed." GT recited the information in an emotionless and matter of fact tone.

"Wait, what do you mean?" Debbie asked. "You said he's laughing at me?"

"Yeah, that's kinda what Zaleos does. He's a demon from Hell. He is capable of lying, but he seems to prefer to tell us really painful truths. Then he laughs at how much those truths hurt us. That's why I don't think he's lying this time. He seems to be far too happy about your situation." GT paused for a moment, as he saw Debbie turn away in pain. "Deborah, I'm sorry. I know that I just upset you."

"What are you talking about? How could you know? What could you possibly know about lesbian relationships?"

"Well, I don't know about that specifically. But I do know that there is always a price to vanquishing a demon. It can be subtle and indirect, but there is always some kind of loss. I have suffered too, I promise you."

"You haven't the first clue what it's like." Debbie said. "I'm still in shock, but I know I'll spend weeks in bed from the loss of the love I felt for May. Already I feel like my heart has been ripped in half. I'm trying to cope, but the pain I feel, it's beyond you."

"I'm sorry, but I do understand pain better than you might think. What happened to me was horrible too." GT spoke without emotion, but Debbie saw hesitation in his eyes.

"Well, what was it then? Just tell me, what happened to you?"

There was a moment of awkward silence as the two stood across from one another on the highway. Then GT spoke. "Mother. My- my mother. I've tried to pretend it never happened. I tried to suppress the memory, but it still haunts me. When I fought Vepar, right before I vanquished him. My mother-." Abruptly GT found himself choked with emotion. To Debbie's astonishment she saw tears streaming down the man's face. She saw his muscular frame shudder with violent sobs. It was an uncanny experience. The man Debbie had grown to respect, who up until now had seemed so stoic and strong. Now that same man was openly weeping right in front of her. Despite her own pain, Debbie did what she felt was right. She took GT in her arms, and held him close.

"It's OK, GT. I understand. It's OK." Debbie repeated the words over and over again. In truth, she didn't understand. Something horrible had happened to GT's mother, she got that much. But GT was sobbing, and Debbie held him even as his tears soaked through the front of her t-shirt. "It's OK, I understand." Debbie said again. She continued to hold him, she continued to comfort him, despite her own pain. She did it because she was a good person. Because that's what she did for her friends.

VALENTINE'S DAY

Unbeknownst to Debbie or GT, the following took place six months earlier:

It was Valentine's Day, and Alex was preparing for his date with Sue. He had set an arrangement of candles around the dinner table and laid out her dish, made of engraved brass, at her place. Alex struck a match and lit the candles one by one. He dimmed the lights, and put the finishing touches on the arrangement. Then he sat down at the table, and took out the cage containing the gift he had bought for her. It was a small hamster, named Peanut.

The candles gleamed in the darkness, throwing a dim light across Alex's face. He looked into the mirror set on the table between the candles. He pulled Peanut from the cage, and placed the hamster gently in the brass dish. Then Alex took a sharp kitchen knife and drew it across Peanut's neck, emptying the small animal's blood into the shallow recess of the dish.

"This small gift of life I give for you, to cherish as you dwell in the beyond. I trust it's significance is apparent." Alex whispered into the mirror. As he sat there in the dark, holding the still warm body of the hamster in his hands, he kept his eyes focused on the dim reflection in the mirror. He saw a brief distortion, as though he was looking into a still pool of water that had suddenly been interrupted by a ripple. Then Sue was there, her face replacing his, staring back at him.

"Of course I recognize its significance." Sue said. She spoke with her mind, rather than her mouth, and her words resonated in his head like a warm caress of soft silk. "You paid money for it, assigning it value. You spent weeks caring for it and showing it affection. You actually feel genuinely sad now that it is dead. All that gives power to its blood, making this a very special gift. It's true when people say it's the thought that counts. Magic begins in your mind."

"I love you, Sue." Alex said. "I wish I could hold you in my arms."

"That's a lie." Sue said, her warm laughter made Alex's heart feel light. "But there's nothing wrong with telling the lady you love a little white lie now and then. It makes us girls feel special."

"You've always understood." Alex smiled. It was true, he wasn't good with physical contact. He had never really understood the obsession other men seemed to have with sex. He wasn't a virgin. Sue had convinced him to see a prostitute once, because it was bad for a man to be a virgin. But the whole thing had left him feeling violated and disgusted. It was gross and smelled funny. The prostitute had seemed to hate him afterwards and he didn't really understand why. He was glad he only had to do it once to not be a virgin anymore, it wasn't something he wanted to do again. But men on TV and in movies always seemed to want to do it. Perhaps he was one of those transgenders he'd heard about, Alex thought to himself. Maybe he was a man who had a woman's mind. All the women on TV seemed to think their partners were stupid and seemed to hate sex as much as he did.

"You don't have a woman's mind." Sue said. She had a habit of knowing what Alex was thinking. "You're just a different kind of man."

"I'm not that different." Alex reminded her. "I used to be able to hug my mother. And I think I might be able to hug you without feeling weird. Maybe if I had some practice to get used to it."

Alex flinched as he heard a sharp pounding at the door of his apartment. He looked back at the mirror but now only his reflection looked back at him. The spell, and his concentration, had been broken. He stood up and walked to the door. Peering through the peephole he saw his landlord, Gabe, on the other side of the door. "What do you want?"

"It's the middle of the month, and I haven't got your rent check yet." Gabe called through the door.

"I wrote you the check. I thought I left it in your mailbox." Even as Alex said this, he started to doubt himself. He did remember writing the check, but he had been busy lately. Had he remembered to drop it off? He went to his raincoat, hanging on the wall nearby, and fished through the pockets. It was there, he had messed up. "Never mind, I found it. I'm slipping it under the door for you."

"It's not just the rent." Gabe said. He made a little grunt as he leaned down to pick up the check. "I want to talk to you."

"So talk." Alex called through the door.

"Can you let me in?" Gabe asked. "I don't really want to do this in the middle of the hallway."

"No." Alex looked at the cooling blood on the brass dish in the dining table. He looked at the dead body of Peanut still in his hand. "I'm sorry, I can't."

"Well how about you just crack the door a little?" Gabe was clearly starting to sound flustered. "I just don't want to yell through the door."

"Ok, just a minute." Alex walked back to the dining table and extinguished the candles. He put Peanut on the bloody dish, and carried it into the small kitchen alcove. Washing his hands off in the sink, Alex then went to his bedroom. He took his jacket out of the closet and slipped it over his head and shoulders. There wasn't much danger in just opening the door to his apartment, he had been thorough when applying the wards around the door frame. But he felt safer covered in his jacket, the additional wards and spells sewn into the inside linings gave him another layer of spiritual protection. Alex walked back to the door of his apartment and slowly began unfastening the locks. In addition to the deadbolt and chain he had drilled in two sets of brackets for additional bolts, one of steel and one of silver. He unfastened these now, leaving only the chain latched, and slowly opened the door.

"Well, I guess this is better than nothing." Gabe said, as he looked at the still fastened chain. "Are you cold, Alex? Why do you have your jacket on like that?"

"Could you make it quick, Gabe?" Alex asked. Even having the door open this wide was starting to make him feel nervous.

"Your Aunt Helen phoned me today. She was worried about you. She said you haven't been picking up the phone."

"I had my phone disconnected." Alex said, rolling his eyes. Ever since his mother had died, Aunt Helen had declared herself Alex's surrogate parent. "What is she doing phoning you?"

"Your aunt and I have been friends since we were kids. She phones me all the time." Gabe said. "She got you this apartment, Alex. She asked me to lease it to you as a favor." The older man tilted his head as he spoke. "Are you having problems remembering things, Alex? Are you taking your medication?"

"I'm almost forty years old." Alex said. "I don't need a babysitter."

"You didn't answer my question, Alex."

"No, I didn't." Alex felt his eyes narrow as he looked past Gabe, to the hallway beyond. There was a shadow cast against the wall, but Alex couldn't determine the light source or object that could create it. He wondered if he was being watched. Certain demons were able to hide their corporeal forms from vision, but it was an imperfect illusion. There was always a way to sniff them out. The easiest would be by performing a scrying.

"I hope you are taking your medicine." Gabe said. "I also wanted to tell you I'll need to enter your apartment tomorrow to check on the plumbing. This is your 24 hours' notice, ok?"

Alex turned his head to the bowl he kept on a stand by the door. He mostly put his loose change there after he went out shopping for groceries. But one of his purple scrying crystals was there too. He reached into the bowl and plucked out the crystal.

"Alex?" Alex's head shot back towards Gabe as the landlord spoke. "Did you hear me?"

"Yes, plumbing problem tomorrow. I got it."

"Fine. I'll see you then." Gabe turned on his heel and walked down the hallway. Alex brought the crystal to his eye and peered through it, but he was too late. The shadow was gone.

Alex felt his teeth clench as he carefully closed and locked the door. He hated having outsiders in his private areas. Gabe was more respectful than most, but even he gave Alex funny looks and asked the odd question. It made Alex feel anxious and interfered with his work. It also meant he would have to tidy some things up. The brass dish would have to be cleaned and polished. Peanut would have to be cut and ground very small so he could be carefully disposed of in the toilet. It was a nasty job, but a necessary one. He didn't want the little guy decomposing in his apartment, it would smell and attract bugs. And if he threw Peanut in the garbage someone might notice it and ask questions. Alex hated answering those kinds of questions.

After spending an hour cleaning up, Alex took the mirror from the dinner table and carried it to his bedroom. He placed it on his desk and powered on his computer. He liked to speak to Sue as he worked. It took a lot of preparation to see her face, but hearing her voice was easier. It wasn't her voice that came from the mirror now, however. Instead, Alex heard a soft squeak. "What the hell is that?" Alex asked.

"That's Peanut, of course." Sue said.

"Peanut is dead." Alex said. "I killed him for you, ground him up, and flushed him down the toilet."

"And now he's with me." Sue said. "His spirit at least. I have him to keep me company."

"So, he'll be squeaking through the mirror at me from now on?"

"You hear squeaking, I hear talking." Sue said.

"Well, what is he saying?" Alex asked.

"He wants to know what you're doing."

"I'm searching online for clues to accessing the Book of Thoth." Alex said. "The text does not exist through this world but I might be able to look at it anyways."

"Peanut wants to know how you'd do that."

"I don't know." Alex said. "But I found out online I can more easily identify demons using quartz scrying stones. And I learned about the different religious symbols I used to ward this apartment with lemon juice. I also learned I could stitch the same symbols into my jacket with scarlet thread. So maybe I can read up on accessing alternate dimensions the same way."

"Isn't Thoth Egyptian? You wouldn't be able to read the book in any case."

"Since when have you discouraged me from pursuing my interests, Sue?" Alex turned to the mirror.

"It's not me talking here, it's Peanut." Sue explained. "For me, I'm only happy when you're happy."

"Fine, well what else does Peanut have to say?"

"He says you have more important things to focus on." Sue said. "The wall of reality is thin tonight, and someone is trying to punch a hole through to allow the demon world access. You have to find out who is doing it and kill him before midnight. You're the only one who can."

Alex felt the hairs on the back of his neck stand on end. "I can't do that. I've never killed someone before. Except Peanut, I suppose. But I don't think he counts."

"There's a first time for everything." Sue said. "You lay with a woman for the first time because I asked you to. This is just a different kind of virginity you need to lose. You will penetrate a man with a blade, instead of a woman with your member. You love me, don't you?"

"Yes, I do."

"Then prove it. Do this for me, for us." Sue said.

"Who is this person, and how do I find him?" Alex asked.

"Peanut doesn't know his name." Sue said. "He knows the person is male, and has a white face with a big brown mark close to his nose. Some sort of birth mark I assume. He should be easy to identify once you see him. Just leave your apartment and walk west."

Alex went to the kitchen cutlery drawer and took out a sharp steak knife. He slipped it carefully into the pocket of his jacket along with Sue's mirror, then he left his apartment. He was careful to close the door behind him. Then he exhaled onto the door, using of the moisture of his breath to reactivate the wards protecting his home from the shadows that crept outside. He checked the lock one more time, then he pulled the hood of his jacket over his scalp and headed out of the building.

"I know what you are, Sue." Alex whispered, as he walked down the street. "It doesn't matter to me, but I know."

"Oh?" Sue asked. "Then what am I?"

"The clue is in your name." Alex said. "Sue, short for succubus."

"Peanut wants to know what a succubus is." Sue teased. "Why don't you tell us what you know."

"One of the most dangerous female demons in existence, the personification of lust." Alex said as he walked. "You are skilled at fulfilling any man's fantasy. You are so beautiful most men find you irresistible. But they are doomed if they cannot resist you."

"Doomed?" Sue said with shy giggle, "How would a man be doomed by me?"

"If he put his..." Alex struggled with the word, "Thing inside of you, it would hurt. You have razor sharp blades and teeth down there that would cut it off or at least mutilate it. And if a man put his mouth there it would be freezing cold and taste disgusting. I mean all women are disgusting down there, but a succubus is a hundred times worse."

"You sure know how to make a girl feel wanted." Sue said. "If I'm so nasty and horrible, why are you with me?"

"Because I don't lust for you." Alex said. "I never want to touch you. I can love you without any kind of dirty feelings getting in the way. I can redeem you with my heart in a way no other man can."

"I'm your damsel in distress." Sue said. Her tone sounded pleased and affectionate. "Please save me, my big strong man, and we'll live happily ever after."

"One thing at a time." Alex said. "I should take care of this guy first." Alex continued to walk west in the cold, dark February night. He wasn't used to strenuous activity, spending most of his time inside, and his legs quickly grew tired. The cold didn't help either, and he began to shiver despite his jacket. Still a promise was a promise, and Alex continued to walk along the city sidewalk.

Alex hadn't brought a watch so he had no idea how long he trudged through the cold darkness of the city. As time wore on, his anxiety increased. He remembered the shadow he had seen in the hallway behind Gabe earlier that day. He had been fairly sure a demon had been following him. Now in the dead of night, there were shadows all around him. Sure, he had warded his jacket with every style of protection he had found online, but there could be others he didn't know about. Besides, demons were skilled at manipulation and theft. If Alex was somehow tricked into removing his jacket, even for a moment, he would be vulnerable to attack. It was much safer in his apartment, behind a thick door and anointed concrete walls. Out here in the open, all at once Alex felt the shadows closing in. He felt a tightness in his chest as anxiety flooded over him, and Alex was overcome with the need to sit down. There was an alley to his right, away from prying eyes, where he could at least put his back to a wall. Alex headed for that.

Upon entering the alley, Alex saw a dumpster that would shield him from direct view of the street. Beside the dumpster, he saw several flattened cardboard boxes. Insulation from the cold ground, Alex thought to himself as he slowly sat down on the cardboard. He would just wait here for a moment until his anxiety passed. Alex drew his knees up to his chest, and wrapped his arms around himself for warmth. He let his chin sink to his chest, and focused on taking deep calming breaths.

A wetness on his cheek brought Alex back to his senses. He yelped and jerked away, bumping his head against the concrete wall as a beagle nuzzled and licked his face. Alex recoiled in disgust, and wiped his hands across his face frantically. He hated being touched, even by a dog.

"That's him." Sue said through the mirror.

"What?" Alex gasped as he continued to wipe the slobber from his face.

"That's who Peanut was talking about." Sue said. "He's obviously male and you can see he has a white face with a large brown spot close to his nose."

"So he does." Alex gently reached out and grabbed the beagle with his left hand. With his right he fished the steak knife out of his pocket. "Is Peanut sure?"

"He's sure." Sue said. "Kill him before he allows the dark ones to invade."

Alex grit his teeth and brought the blade to the dog's neck. He had hoped to make it quick and painless, but he had never killed something this big before. The beagle squirmed in his arms and Alex saw his victim's eyes go wide with panic. He heard his victim yelp in pain as he applied more pressure to the knife. It penetrated the beagle's neck and blood bubbled around the blade. It was warm and wet, and there was a lot more of it than Alex had assumed there would be. It made a mess of his hands, jacket, and pants. But eventually the beagle stopped struggling and the deed was done.

"That's it." Sue said in a soothing voice. "You might not appreciate it now, given the mess you've made. And your deeds will remain unknown to the world at large. Still, you saved the world tonight and everyone in it."

"I just want to go home now." Alex said, as he let the dead beagle drop from his hands. "I don't feel well." He slipped the bloody knife into the pocket of his jeans, and began the slow walk back to his apartment. It was 3:20am when he finally returned home. He was too tired to bother with anything other than the deadbolt lock, but he was careful to secure the wards with the moisture of his breath. The wards were what really kept the demons out. Alex knew he should clean the dried blood off of his clothes, but he was already exhausted. It was all he could do to slip out of his clothes, leaving them in a heap on the floor. Naked, Alex crawled into his bed, and slipped into a dreamless sleep.

"What did you do?" Gabe shook Alex violently as he spoke. "What did you do, Alex?"

"Gabe?" Alex blinked the grogginess from his eyes. "What are you doing here?"

"You know why I'm here." Gabe said. "I gave you a day's notice so I could come in and check the plumbing. Why are there bloody clothes and a dirty knife by the door? Did you stab someone?"

"I had to." Alex said. "Sue's hamster said if I didn't kill him the world would end." Alex could tell by the look on Gabe's face he had made a mistake. Sue had warned him this would happen. His good deed would remain unknown, people wouldn't understand.

"Your aunt was right." Gabe said. "We can't leave you by yourself. You need real help. Stay here." Gabe turned and began walking out of the bedroom.

Alex looked to his bedside table, where he normally kept Sue's mirror. It wasn't there. He must have left it in his jacket. Alex sprang from his bed and rushed past Gabe to the pile of clothes. He reached into the jacket pocket and felt his hand grip the mirror. It was then that Alex realized he was still naked. He turned and saw an even more horrified expression on Gabe's face.

"You were going for your knife, weren't you?" Gabe said, holding the blood-stained steak knife up for Alex to see. "Did you think I'd just leave it there?"

"He's going to take away your freedom, Alex." Sue whispered through the mirror. "That knife is evidence. You have to get it back."

"Give me the knife, Gabe." Alex said. "Just drop it and walk away. Forget you saw anything."

"That's crazy, I can't do that." Gabe said. "I'm partly responsible for you. I promised your aunt."

Alex took a step toward Gabe, holding out his hand. "Just ignore this." Alex said. "It's not your problem." All at once Alex saw fear in Gabe's eyes, and the old man made a dash for the door. Alex made a move of his own, catching his landlord in a tackle that brought them both crashing to the ground. Alex heard a crack as he landed, and saw that the mirror had shattered under his weight. "Give me the knife, Gabe." Alex repeated, his voice choked as tears began to form in his eyes.

But Gabe didn't answer, and as Alex looked closer, he realized why. Gabe had been holding the steak knife in front of him as he had fallen, and the point was buried up to the handle in the old man's chest. Fresh blood now joined with the dried blood on the handle of the knife, and Alex knew that the man was dead.

"It's ok." Alex heard Sue's voice echo faintly through the shattered fragments of her mirror. "He's with me now. I'll take care of him the same way I took care of Peanut. You just need to clean up the mess."

Alex took the body of his landlord in his arms, and carried him to the bathroom. He'd let the old man bleed out in the tub, then he'd cut the body very small and grind it up so it would go down the toilet. It was a nasty job, but a necessary one. He didn't want the big guy decomposing in his apartment. It would attract bugs and smell. And Alex couldn't just dump it in the trash. Someone might notice and ask Alex questions. Alex hated answering those kinds of questions.

ASTAROTH'S FORTY LEGIONS

1 Alantus Anguis aka Narcotic Serpent: A large snake with feathered wings and protruding fangs. Capable of flight. Its fangs secrete a venomous narcotic strong enough to incapacitate adult victims. Will often unhinge its jaw and consume said victims, unless ordered otherwise. Prone to salt, flame and conventional weapons.

2 Apis Levo aka Air Lifter: Resembling a large insect, thirty feet long and six feet wide. It has an angular head sporting four eyes, two large and two small. It sports a tubular torso resembling a large, black, hollow balloon. Has four red wings like that of a dragonfly and six thin elongated limbs below its belly. These unnaturally long limbs can grasp heavy material, such as Tenebris Ferrum, and lift it to great heights. Not immediately hostile, will flee if attacked. Prone to water, silver and salt.

3 Artus Conflata aka Fused Torsos: What appears to be a collection of severed human body parts fused back together into a mass roughly six feet in diameter. Will attempt to strangle or blind the eyes of humans it encounters. Prone to conventional weapons and flame.

4 Avibus Nox aka Dark Cathartid: Like a large vulture, but lacking feathers and having a bat's wings. Will fly in a group of six. Prone to

silver and flame. Can be injured and incapacitated with conventional weapons.

5 Belial Lupal aka Hell Hounds: Resembles a hairless wolf, but with clawed hands in place of paws, and two additional crablike limbs. Prone to conventional weapons and flame.

6 Cacophaton Cantor aka Persistent Shrieker: A large wormy demon, rooted to the ground, crowned with the face of a young man. Sways side to side in a rhythmic pattern, shrieking sustained notes. To the human ear it sounds like a constant scream of pain, but to demons it is soothing music. Will spawn in loose soil with a high nitrogen content, but can be uprooted and planted in other sections of earth. Prone to silver, salt, and flame.

7 Caducus Intellectus aka Fragile Calculators: Short demons vaguely resembling humans. They have oversized heads, unnaturally thin torsos and spindly limbs. Able to speak, known to make quick and precise calculations. Hell has no computers, instead relying on such demons to handle complex math. Prone to conventional weapons, silver and salt.

8 Cera Crucifixio aka Wax Crucifixion: Appears to be a melted wax figure of a man displayed spread eagle and upside down on flat surfaces. Presumably intended as a debasement of the crucifixion of Saint Peter. Is immobile but will emit a low moan. At intervals, Inanis Campe/Vain Wind will burst from a cavity in its chest. Also secretes small quantities of Fraus Unda from its eyes. Prone to water.

9 Cruor Concordia aka Crimson Consonance: Clusters of red snakes slithering in a dense swarm. They can cling to sheer surfaces and share a hive mind. They are nonvenomous, but will bite flesh from their victims in turns until an entire body is consumed. Prone to salt and flame.

10 Curiosus Salax Miles aka The Lady in the Shadows: Demon that looks like a woman. She has the eyes of a cat and feet twisted backwards

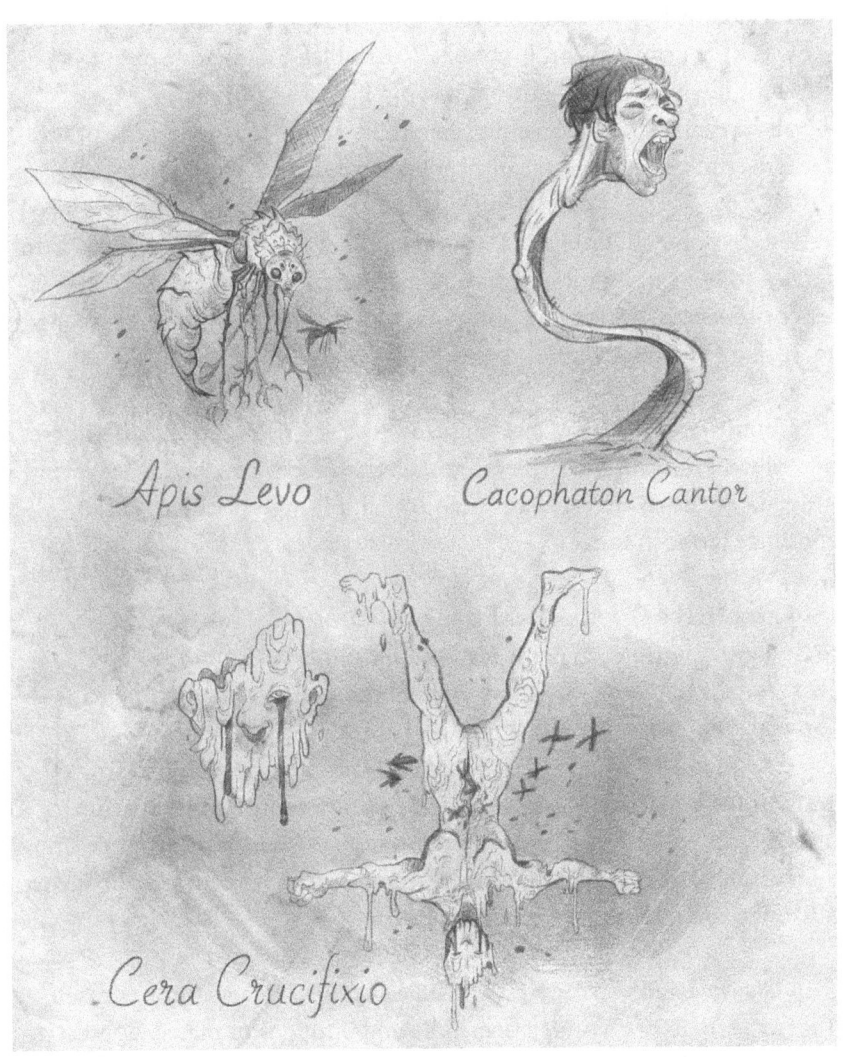

Apis Levo

Cacophaton Cantor

Cera Crucifixio

at the ankle. Seems to specialize at emotional manipulation, feeding into one's desire to nurture and protect a vulnerable woman. Weak to conventional weapons.

11 Dabidus Praebitor aka Meat Plant: Spawns from an advanced growth of Muco Daemon Involuta. Resembles a stumpy brown tree, but with flexible worms slowly growing in place of branches. These worms are toxic to humans but seem to be edible to some of the other demons, providing a source of protein. Prone to salt and flame.

12 Daemon Arachnid aka Demonic Spider: Vaguely looks like a giant spider. Has a gaping mouth, sporadic eyes and long limbs. Secretes tenebris ferrum, a sticky building material that hardens to be as strong as steel. Prone to silver.

13 Equus Tabidus aka Decaying Horse: Very similar to Earth's horses, but with significantly more eyes and teeth. Also sports a long slavering tongue. Prone to silver. Can be poisoned if it ingests salt, or if salt enters its bloodstream.

14 Erat Herba Praefoco aka Strangulation Weed: What appears to be a green mound of plant material. From this mound extends two tendrils that seek out and strangle potential victims. Prone to conventional weapons, silver, salt and flame.

15 Fraus Unda aka False Liquid: A corrosive sentient liquid that increases in volume as it consumes biomass. Also used as a source of nourishment or building material by more advanced demons. Prone to salt and flame. Can also dry out on its own.

16 Glasya-Labolas: A count of Hell's peerage, a legion unto himself. Takes the form of a winged dog. The embodiment of manslaughter, is impulsive and violent. The peerage can be hurt but not killed by silver. While serving Astaroth, will dissolve if it's Pituita Cortex is peeled away.

17 Graviditate Odium aka Horrific Parturiency: A fourteen foot tall humanoid demon that constantly gestates a fetus in its belly. It will intermittently birth this fetus, expelling it upon the ground where it will die and dissolve into Muco Daemon Involuta and Fraus Unda. Prone to silver and flame.

18 Harpy: One of the few demons known to the general public, due to Greek tradition. Wings, legs and talons of a giant bird of prey, torso of a fit attractive woman, head of an ugly ancient crone. Weak to fire, salt and silver.

19 Hominum Incognita aka The Faceless Man: A motionless statue lacking a face. It speaks with the voice of a loved one and will attempt forms of emotional manipulation and try to overwhelm you with guilt. Fragile and easily destroyed by conventional weapons.

20 Immanis Colosseus aka The Colossal Monstrosity: Air version is a giant feathered bird, only in place of a head there is a giant hole at the stump of its neck lined with teeth and a large slavering tongue. Huge size necessitates huge caloric intake to remain active. Needs to consume large quantities of protein to have the energy to flap its wings. If unable to feed, will remain grounded until fully fed. Vulnerable to salt and silver.

21/22 Incubus/Succubus: One of the few demons known to the general public. Can use emotional manipulation, but specializes in manipulating sexual desire. Weak to silver.

23 Inanis Campe aka Vain Wind. These are mothlike demons with razor sharp wings. They manifest in the chest cavity of the Cera Crucifixio in a swarm of 35, sharing a single consciousness or hivemind. They are prone to fire and salt.

24 Lacertae Homines aka Lizard men: Reptilian creatures that stand 5 feet tall and have the ability to grasp simple tools and weapons. Have the same general strength as a man but less intelligent. Weak to conventional weapons and fire.

25 Lightning/Thunder Bird, a black and white demon closely resembling a large feathered bird. It intermittently emits flashes of light and cracks resembling thunder with the flap of its wings. It has a taste for human blood. Weak to silver and salt. Driven back by flames.

26 Lues Volucris aka Baneful Swarm: A swarm of small insectoid demons that gather in groups of 20-50. Emit a distinct shriek, similar to a red fox. Will relentlessly bite and scratch. Prone to salt and flame.

27 Malae Turbela aka Sinister Swarm: Appearing like swarms of overgrown winged maggots, these demons will converge and consume a human body in under a minute. Prone to flame.

28 Malphas: A count of Hell's peerage, a legion unto himself. Appears as part man, part raven. Known as a builder, capable of long-term planning and deception. The peerage can be hurt but not killed by silver. While serving Astaroth, will dissolve if its Pituita Cortex is peeled away.

29 Muco Daemon Involuta aka Hell's Fungus: Demonic fungal tissue that provides nesting areas and nourishment for more advanced demons. Prone to salt, flame, and strong alcohol.

30 Murex Tartarus aka Tartarean Stone: A twenty-foot-tall stone demon. Spawns Lues Volucris and Fraus Unda. Prone to high yield explosives and silver.

31 Nebula Caligo aka Drifting Shades: Demons that appear through shadows, invisible to the naked eye. Can be seen through certain anointed crystals, like amethyst or selenite. They do not attack, instead they gather information for more powerful demons of the peerage as

Inanis Campe *Lacertae Homines*

Parvulus Hirudo

spies. Driven off by bright light and flame. Obstructed by salt or lemon juice. Intense ultra violet light can destroy it, if directly applied for several seconds.

32 Opprimo Cantharidas aka Monstrous Beetles. Large black insectoid demons capable of flight and roughly the size of a fist, with mandibles capable of tearing flesh from bone. Noted for using human bones to construct nests to gestate more of its spawn. Prone to silver and flame.

33 Ora Seriem aka Constricted Gnashers: A floating oval membrane that surrounds a pocket of darkness filled with mouths of sharp teeth. Prone to puncture from conventional penetrating weapons.

34 Parvulus Hirudo aka Nascent Leech: Tiny airborne parasites. Appearing to the naked eye as little more than a rainbow tinted mist, these small demon organisms operate with a hivemind. They penetrate on contact, consume blood for nourishment to gestate into larger Malae Turbela. Prone to water and flame.

35 Pinguis Vermis aka Tendrilled Worm: A four-foot-long wormlike demon with six small tendrilled limbs. It sports a mouth of jagged teeth that will specifically target a victim's stomach. This demon is known for consuming a victim's intestines. Prone to silver.

36 Praemunitus Ales aka Winged Lancer: While contracted, resembles a giant tailless scorpion. When startled by high frequency sound, will unfurl wings and hop back four feet. Prone to silver, explosives, flame.

37 Putridus Pegasus aka Corrupted Pegasus: General body of a horse, but tentacles in place of legs, wings like a bat, and a large wormy appendage in place of a head. Weak to silver, salt, and fire.

38 Secretio Laterem aka Brick Maker: Resembling a large stone head, with a fanged mouth for an opening. Spawns from a developed

foundation of Muco Daemon Involuta. Is fed Fraus Unda and
Protein. Secretes copious amounts of Tenebris Ferrum, a malleable
demonic material that hardens over time. This material is used in the
construction of large objects, such as buildings or nests. Prone to water
(dissolves on contact) and large amounts of salt.

39 Sicco Lolligo aka Dry Squid: Resembles a three-foot-tall land
bound squid. It will glide along the ground on its tendrils, but push
itself into the air with the ability to jump distances of up to 30 feet. It
has venomous barbs that paralyze on contact. Its vision appears limited,
it is not always accurate in its jumps. Prone to water and salt.

40 Timendus Lus aka Dreadful Light: Resembles a three-foot-long
caterpillar. Emits an odourless gas that seems to slightly affect one's
perception of light. This causes slight disorientation and a strong sense
of unease in humans. Is also believed to enhance the orange glow of
Astaroth's corruption. Seems to create an environment that is more
appealing to demons of the air. Prone to conventional weapons, silver,
salt, and flame.

Putridus Pegasus

Secretio Laterem

Sicco Lolligo

AUTHOR'S NOTE

The following discussion took place during the planning of this book:

Author: I have this crazy idea for a novel. I've been thinking a lot about exploitative lesbian pulp novels from the 50s. I thought it'd be fun to write a book inspired by that genre. Give the book the craziest title ever, like "Lesbian Biker Babes from Transylvania vs The Air Demons of Hell." But I'd actually write the book to be a nuanced and respectful examination of a lesbian character without any real fetishization or exploitation.

Peer: The title would drive away potential female readers, and potential male readers would feel betrayed by the content. Who would this book be for?

Author: Well, it'd actually be about fighting demons. I'd make it part of my "Infernal Legions" series.

Peer: Don't you think Lesbian groups would be upset, given you'd kinda be using them for shock value?

Author: I think if they read the novel, they'd understand my intentions and see where I was coming from. I mean, the whole point is to provide a hero for queer girls who might be looking for representation. They can read about the protagonist, see what she's going through, apply that to their own lives. Maybe feel less alone when they see elements of themselves reflected in my book. Ultimately the idea of having a queer female hero is to give the readers someone to look up to. I'm hoping that anyone who reads my book in depth will get that kind of idea.

Peer: There's a book called "Hansi, the Girl Who Loved the Swastika." It's a true account of a Czech orphan indoctrinated into the Hitler Youth. It's a nuanced story of her dealing with the fall of Germany, the horrors of her experiences in a Russian prison camp, and her escape and eventual relocation into America. Most people ignore all of that and just focus on the title that describes a girl loving a swastika. They just assume the book is Nazi propaganda.

Author: I'm not writing about Nazis.

Peer: Change the title, you idiot!

Congratulations on completing *Astaroth's Infernal Legions*.

We would love if you could help by posting a review at
your book retailer and on the PageMaster Publishing
site. It only takes a minute and it would really help
others by giving them an idea of your experience.

Thanks

To order more copies of this book, find books by other
Canadian authors, or make inquiries about publishing
your own book, contact PageMaster at:

PageMaster Publication Services Inc.
11340-120 Street, Edmonton, AB T5G 0W5
books@pagemaster.ca
780-425-9303

catalogue and e-commerce store
PageMasterPublishing.ca/Shop